⏻FFLINE

ALSO BY DONNA COONER

Fake
Screenshot
Worthy
Can't Look Away
Skinny

OFFLINE

DONNA COONER

POINT

ISBN 978-1-338-58514-8

1 2020

Printed in the U.S.A. 23

First edition, September 2020

Book design by Yaffa Jaskoll

For Karmen

LUNA: GOOD MORNING! UP AND AT 'EM, PEEPS!

CAITLIN: UGH! DON'T BE SO PEPPY. I'M TIRED . . .

ANNIE: THAT'S WHAT TOO MUCH EXERCISE DOES TO A PERSON.

CAITLIN: THAT COULD BE. *GETS BACK INTO BED*

ANNIE: *SENDS VIRTUAL COFFEE*

LUNA: UM, YOU GUYS KNOW IT'S A SCHOOL DAY, RIGHT? MY MOM IS DRIVING ME IN EARLY FOR MY EMERGENCY NEWSPAPER MEETING.

ANNIE: I KNOW, I KNOW. I'M TRYING TO DO MY MAKEUP BEFORE JAMESON GETS HERE.

CAITLIN: DID YOU SEE THE MAKEUP VIDEO MARIAH POSTED ON CHITCHAT LAST NIGHT?

ANNIE: SERIOUSLY. THAT GIRL NEVER SLEEPS. 1 IN THE MORNING AND SHE'S

PUTTING ON LIPSTICK?? OVER AND OVER
AGAIN?

CAITLIN: AND MORE IMPORTANTLY, WHY???

LUNA: YOU GUYS WERE WATCHING,
SO . . . DUH

ANNIE: OUCH *TAKES KNIFE OUT OF HEART*

LUNA: PULLING UP TO SCHOOL NOW. GOT TO
GO.

CAITLIN: AM GETTING OUT OF BED FOR
REAL.

ANNIE: JAMESON IS OUTSIDE HONKING. SEE
YOU TWO LATER. ♥

CHAPTER ONE

If you're brave enough to say goodbye, life will reward you with a new hello.

—Paulo Coelho

"Stop honking!" I called, stepping out of my house and closing the front door behind me. I waved frantically until my boyfriend, Jameson, held his hands up over the steering wheel in surrender. I tucked my ruffled plaid top into my zip-ring denim skirt with one hand, while balancing my phone, book bag, and a sweater in the other. "I'm coming."

My neighbor Mrs. Miron was walking her dog past my house, and she stopped with a scowl. Lulu, the pit bull by her side, looked just as unhappy. But then Lulu always looked like that. Honestly, I'm not a big fan. Of dogs, or Mrs. Miron.

"Sorry!" I said. Mrs. Miron and her pit bull just glared back at me.

I slid into the passenger side and slammed the door of the beat-up Chevy SUV. Throwing my bag into the back seat, I looked over at Jameson. He had sunglasses on and his mouth was set in a straight grim line. I wondered if the sunglasses were to keep me from reading his expression. I could still tell he was in a bad mood. Not the best way to start a Monday.

I flipped down the mirror on the visor and rubbed away smudges of mascara from under my left eye that never would have been there if he had not rushed me. I brushed off the thought and put a big grin on my face.

"Good morning," I chirped, trying to channel the same energy my best friend, Luna, always displayed. "Did you know it is three o'clock in the afternoon right now in Paris?"

"What's your point?" Jameson asked, still facing straight ahead.

"If we were in Paris, you'd be over your morning grumps and we would be sipping hot cocoa in some outdoor café."

He responded with something like a grunt. Jameson was *not* a morning person. Neither was my other best friend, Caitlin, but she wasn't quite as grouchy about it.

"We're not in Paris," Jameson mumbled, then put the car in reverse. "Obviously."

I shrugged it off. Even though Colorado was definitely not Paris, it was still a beautiful morning. A burst of fall colors engulfed the trees on Mainsail Drive and a cool late-September chill made me slip on my black cardigan with a shiver.

Plenty of people travel to visit Colorado every year, I told myself. *We should feel lucky we live here.*

"Photo op," I said, then leaned over to take a selfie of us. Jameson's blond hair, still damp from the shower, curled around the neck of his navy-blue T-shirt and he smelled faintly like mint. Probably from the shower gel I bought him for his birthday in August. He still didn't smile, but when I glanced down at the photo, I thought that only made him look cooler. Besides, I knew that, even on Jameson's crankiest of mornings, we looked good together. Everybody said so.

Caitlin and Luna constantly teased me about my romanticized view of the world, but I didn't care. I liked happy endings and the idea of finding someone who made your toes curl up in your shoes. When I started high school, I kept picturing myself with a boyfriend. Walking the halls hand in hand with a boy. Dancing to slow songs. Laughing at movies in the dark. Kissing.

And now I had all that with Jameson. We'd been together since last fall—almost a full year. And maybe it could be a little annoying, but I liked showing off our happiness on social media. Getting all those likes and comments somehow made our relationship feel stronger.

I studied our selfie. Jameson looked great, as always, but even though I'd pushed my chin out and angled my face in just the right way, my cheekbones had disappeared into the roundness of my face.

I quickly added a rabbit filter to the photo. The pink nose with the big whiskers hid part of my face—which was good—but I knew I was using way too many filters lately. It was becoming a habit designed to camouflage and conceal. People were bound to comment on it.

I blinked hard.

The truth was, I wanted to hide more than my face. Lately, it was as though my body craved to be bigger, rounder, and take up more space. My dress sizes kept going up. That was the reason I'd started posting pictures of my latest pedicures on ChitChat. Toes stayed the same size even when I didn't. Where were the filters for curvier hips and wider thighs?

Maybe if I were more like Caitlin, constantly moving and always competing with someone, the weight would stay away. Earlier in the fall, for the first time, I overheard two girls talking about me in the hall at school. One said in a fake kind voice how sad it was that I was getting fat because I had *such a pretty face.*

Like fat and pretty couldn't possibly go together.

I let my breath out in a long sigh, then posted the altered photo on ChitChat with the hashtags #schooldaze #cutie #2cool4school #Annson.

I'd come up with that special hashtag that combined our names—Annie and Jameson—last year, and it stuck. Whenever people posted pictures or videos of me and Jameson, they used that same hashtag. Jameson rolled his eyes at it, but I secretly loved that it made us seem like celebrities.

"You're always late," Jameson muttered, the sudden comment jolting me away from my screen. "That's why I had to honk, okay?"

I glanced up from my phone. He used to think it was cute when I was late. Now, not so much.

"But I'm worth the wait, right?" I teased.

He shrugged, and I finally saw a hint of a smile.

Jameson turned the corner at the light and headed around the lake. I stared out the window at the geese on the water, thinking how only two months ago Jameson and I were paddleboarding right at that very spot. I'd posted an amazing picture on ChitChat of Jameson standing on the board, his arms spread wide. The sunset had peeked through the foothills behind him, surrounding his body with a warm golden glow. It was the perfect burst of summer in one photo. The pink of the sky. The yellow of the paddleboard. The reflected mountains in the blue water. And Jameson, looking like a professional model, all blond curls and wet, lean muscles. It was easy to come up with the right hashtags. #rockymountainhunk #lakeday #summervibes

Now I scrolled through my feed to find the photo. I smiled. *There. This* was the Jameson I loved. Not that I didn't love him in all seasons, but seriously, summer Jameson was the best. Everybody agreed with me because that image was one of my most popular posts. It even got a like from one of my favorite ChitChat travel influencers, @WaywardChild. Of course, I'd tagged her intentionally in the post so she would notice. But still. It worked.

I glanced up from my phone. The geese took off in a sudden cloud, and I wondered what made them decide all at once to leave. Did they ever lose their ability to stop following the crowd?

"I can't believe the lake will be covered in ice in only a few more months," I said. "I wish it was still summer."

"But then you wouldn't have any place to show off that new skirt," Jameson said.

He noticed. I liked that, but I couldn't help thinking he didn't say the skirt looked good. I debated about whether or not to ask him, but kept quiet. Needy was never a good look on anyone.

"But there is *one* plus about the fall," I said, then waited. He didn't respond. "The Fall Festival," I went on. "Discord will be playing there."

"*If* we get the gig," Jameson said.

Jameson was the guitar player and lead singer for Discord. The band just formed last year, but they had a great sound and some real talent. And that's exactly what I'd told student council president Cheri Thomas when she'd started planning the Fall Festival earlier this month. On my recommendation, she'd asked Discord to audition to be the Festival band, and that audition was coming up soon.

I had no doubt Discord would get the gig. They'd been playing at coffee shops, but the Fall Festival was a real show. The whole school was going to freak out when they heard them, and I was going to be right there in the wings cheering Jameson on.

"Can you get a ride home from Caitlin today?" Jameson asked, his eyes on the road. "Or Luna?"

"Well, not Caitlin," I said. My car situation changed when my older sister, Savanna, moved back home for college. Now we had to coordinate who got the one car we shared between the two of us. "Caitlin's dad drives her, so she has to wait after school until he finishes football practice."

"Oh, right," Jameson said. "I forgot."

That was weird. No one forgot Caitlin's dad was the varsity football coach for Fort Collins High School. It was like being the daughter of a movie star. Especially this year, when the team was predicted to go all the way to the district championship. Caitlin herself was the star of the girls' soccer team, but their season was in the spring.

"I'll ask Luna, though," I said, firing a quick text off to her. There was no immediate answer, but that wasn't a surprise. I knew she was at her newspaper meeting.

The three of us—Luna, Caitlin, and me—grew up in the same cookie-cutter neighborhood. With the windows open in the summer, our houses were close enough to hear everything—phone rings, baby cries, dog barks, and even angry arguments. Caitlin always said we were either going to be best friends or mortal enemies. Thank God we turned out to be best friends. Inseparable since the start, we spent most of our childhood climbing over the low wooden fences of our yards and into the shared space in back of the houses. We went to grade school together. Then middle school, and now high school.

"What are you doing this afternoon?" I asked Jameson. "Are you rehearsing with Discord?"

The beat of silence after my question made me look up from my phone.

"I have plans," Jameson finally said, his eyes not leaving the road.

I waited for him to elaborate, but that was it. Not wanting to make him even grumpier, I didn't ask for any further explanation. Besides, he would probably tell me all about it later when he was in a better mood. We had no secrets.

The red lights flashed ahead at the train crossing, and Jameson mumbled under his breath when we slowed to a stop behind a line of cars waiting for the gates to go back up.

"I can have friends, too, you know," he said after a moment.

It was as though he was having a conversation in his head and suddenly decided to include me in it partway through.

"Of course you can have friends," I said.

"You hang out all the time with Luna and Caitlin."

"Of course I do." I frowned. Jameson never seemed to mind before that Caitlin, Luna, and I were all so close.

Where is this coming from? Why is he being weird? "But you can hang out with us, too."

"They aren't my friends. Not really. They're yours. They always have been."

I was shocked. "How can you say that?"

"The only reason they are friends with me is because of you," Jameson said. "If you were gone, they'd be gone."

"Gone where? I'm not planning on going anywhere."

"Yes, you are. You're always planning . . . and dreaming about leaving here." He didn't sound angry, just matter-of-fact. And he was right. We both knew my ChitChat feed was filled to the brim with travel photos from all over the world. It was no secret I dreamed of jungles, beaches, cliffs, and sunsets. But mostly I dreamed of sharing them all with Jameson.

"I want to see the world, but I'll always want to come home."

"It doesn't matter," he finally muttered.

The conversation hit a dead end. I chewed on the nail of my little finger and looked down at my phone, my immediate response to escaping any awkward conversation or situation. Luna had written back to say she couldn't give me a ride that afternoon because she had to do newspaper stuff. She'd added a bunch of sad-face emojis to show she was sorry. I sent a kissing face back to show I understood.

Jameson pulled into the school parking lot and found a space on the final row out by the tennis courts. He got out first and headed toward the building. I grabbed my bag, slammed the door, and then hurried to catch up with him. When we first met in middle school, I was almost a head taller than him. Now the top of my head barely reached his shoulder. We'd both changed.

Two freshman girls turned to look at us, then whisper-giggled as they walked by. I should have been used to it by now, but popularity via boyfriend was something I would never understand.

Usually, Jameson and I walked into school holding hands. But today we didn't. And that—that last moment of weirdness after the whole weird car ride—gave me a pit in my stomach. Maybe Jameson wasn't just in a grumpy mood because it was morning. Maybe there was something else going on. But before I could ask him what was wrong, the bell rang and we went our separate ways to class.

CHAPTER TWO

It is not easy to find happiness in ourselves, and it is not possible to find it elsewhere.

—Agnes Repplier

Nobody should have geometry first period. Brains need to warm up before diving into theorems concerning triangle properties. But Ms. Garcia was way into it all, with a perkiness that tried to make the Pythagorean theorem sound ah-ma-zing.

I wasn't buying it.

Iain McCloud was a center on the football team and sat in front of me. His huge shoulders were the perfect block to shield my phone from Ms. Garcia's view.

I checked ChitChat and saw a new post from Luna—a picture of the journalism room, with its computers lined up just waiting for reporters to hop on and churn out the next big story. Her caption read: #thisiswhereithappens #breakingnews.

When Luna was eight, she wrote her first news story. It was an interview with one of our neighbors, Mr. Sanderson, about his garage break-in. The "robber" had turned out to be Mrs. Miron's pit bull, Lulu, who lived across the street. So Luna tossed in some flying pigs, a magic shoe, and a garage door opener that led to a different dimension to make the article a bit more exciting. I watched her care-fully write *Luna Ortega, age 8,* on the top right-hand corner of the article, then crumple the piece of paper into a ball and throw it in the trash.

Luna said it was a very bad news story, but I knew it was only the start. I waited until she left her room to go use the bathroom, then dug the story out of the trash can and carefully smoothed out the wrinkled paper. I stashed the article in my backpack and took it home, because I knew the day would come that Luna would be a famous journalist and everyone would want to see how she began her career. And now, seven years later, she was on her way.

Ms. Garcia clapped loudly at the front of the room in an attempt to wake up her audience. Iain McCloud jerked awake in front of me, his head bobbing back as he made a loud yelp-ing noise. I felt an intense desire to laugh, but managed to muffle it with a cough. I clamped my hand over my twitch-ing mouth. Now was not the time to come down with a fit of the giggles and draw Ms. Garcia's attention. I swallowed hard, trying to gain control. Then I returned my focus to my phone and sent a quick text to Caitlin.

ME: RIDE HOME TODAY? AFTER SCHOOL?

CAITLIN: YES BUT U HAVE TO COME TO FOOTBALL PRACTICE

ME: OK ☹

CAITLIN: AT LEAST U CAN KEEP ME
COMPANY.

Ms. Garcia cleared her throat. I looked up quickly
and then, seeing a frown on her face, turned my phone
over on the desk. When it buzzed again, I ignored it, but
it wasn't easy. What if it was Jameson, texting me to say he
was sorry for how he'd acted in the car? I still felt unsettled at the memory of how distant he'd been.

"Okay. Who brought in an example from last night's
homework to challenge us all?" Ms. Garcia asked in her
most authoritative boss voice, trying to break through the
brick wall of silence. Ms. Garcia was one of the youngest
teachers in the school, and one of the most stylish. Today
her thick black hair was clipped back with three tiny but-
terfly pins that matched the flowers on her dress. But still,
she managed to seem intimidating. "Go."

Kacie Barrette—perky, petite, and too perfect—jumped
up immediately to go to the whiteboard. She carefully
drew two triangles on the board, then said, "Triangle A
prime, B prime, C prime is the image of triangle ABC.
Determine the angle of rotation."

She stepped to the side and waited for the brilliance
to flow freely from the blank faces staring back at her.
Seriously? I almost groaned out loud. When no one
answered, Ms. Garcia started lecturing us about paying
attention.

I snuck another peek at my phone, hoping to see that

apology text from Jameson. Instead, it was just a text from Caitlin of a football emoji. Great.

○   ○   ○

"Can you close your locker?" Caitlin asked me. We'd met up right after first period at our lockers. Luna would be here any minute. "It's blocking my view."

"He isn't going anywhere." I pulled one more book out, glancing at the mirror on the inside of my locker door. My hair was a disaster. I tucked one dirty-blond strand behind my ear and grimaced at my reflection. If only filters existed in real life.

"Who are we looking at?" Luna asked, walking up to join us. Her long, curly dark hair was in a side fishtail braid I knew took her an extra hour of prep time. She wore tights, a bright blue skirt, and a too-big gray hoodie. Of the three of us, I thought she was the true beauty, even though most people looked at me first. She had dark perceptive eyes, light brown skin, and the kind of big, confident smile that I always wished I could flash, too. Caitlin was slim and deceptively fragile-looking, with skin so pale it was almost translucent, hazel eyes, and wavy brown hair. Today, she wore jeans and a chunky cropped sweater that showed off her toned stomach. People always thought Caitlin was younger than she actually was, which was hilarious, because Cait was actually older than both me and Luna by almost a year.

I jerked my head toward the end of the hall, where a

gaggle of admirers surrounded Milo Moretti. The football team had been ecstatic when Milo moved here from California this fall and majorly upped their chances of a winning season. Evidently, he had some mad skills and was so fast even the coach couldn't believe the stopwatch in his hand. At least that's what Cait said, and she knew everything about football. And now *everyone* in the school thought Milo was the coolest.

I thought I heard murmurs from the crowd around him talking about a "big party tonight," but I couldn't be sure. It would be just like Milo to throw a party on a school night.

"We're hate-watching Milo," Caitlin explained. "Look at his fans hanging on to his every word." She rolled her eyes.

"You're just jealous," Luna said.

Caitlin considered. "Probably. You'll never see anyone from the girls' soccer team getting that kind of attention."

She was right. I watched the Milo show for a few more minutes, then turned back to my locker and dug around in the bottom for a hair tie. The pink one would do, although it didn't match anything I was wearing. I slipped it around my wrist for later when my hair felt overpowering and unmanageable. It was bound to happen after lunch.

"Did you see his latest ChitChat post?" Caitlin asked, waving her phone. I closed my locker and turned around to look at Caitlin's screen. Milo's post was a photo of himself in midair, catching a pass in the end zone, from last week's game. I saw that Jameson had commented beneath it with a "100" emoji. I knew Jameson really wanted to be Milo's friend. The thought of Jameson made my stomach clench. I still hadn't heard from him, and he usually texted me by now.

"Okay, but let's talk about something more important," Luna said. She gave a big puff of air to clear her face of random strands of hair that had escaped from her braid. "Tamar called that emergency newspaper meeting this morning because she's *moving* next month."

"She's leaving?" Caitlin asked, surprised. Tamar was the editor in chief of the newspaper, and Luna had always looked up to her.

Luna nodded, her expression serious. "And she needs a new editor in chief to replace her." Luna put a hand over her heart, then said, "If I become editor in chief, I can finally tell important stories about things that matter. Stories that can change people's lives."

"That's amazing," I said, knowing how much this meant to Luna. "How is she going to choose the new editor in chief?"

Luna looked nervous. She always wore her expressions easily on her face. "Well, our assignment is to write the best story we can on a topic of our choosing, and submit it to Tamar at the end of October. She'll choose based on whomever submits the best story."

"You totally got this," Caitlin said, and I nodded.

"What are you going to write about?" I asked.

Luna smiled. "I have one idea. A bunch of desks are piled up outside the band room, yet people are having to share desks in English class."

Caitlin frowned. "There's a desk conspiracy?"

Luna shrugged. "Could be."

"Why would anyone hoard desks?" Caitlin asked, bewildered.

"Never mind." Luna's happy look was gone. "Maybe that's not the best idea."

"You'll come up with something great," I assured her.

Luna looked unconvinced. "But what if I don't?" she asked.

"You will," I said, and I held out my fist for our traditional three-way fist bump. "You can do anything you set your mind to."

And I believed it, too. I only wished I could be as sure of myself as I was of my friends.

○   ○   ○

After school, Caitlin and I sat on a metal bench listening to Cait's dad yell at high school boys. When we were about twelve, I realized for the first time that Caitlin's father was not like other fathers. Her dad was Coach Stone. Not the part-time, summer-league kind of coach with a regular job at the bank. No, her dad was a *real* coach—the head football coach at Fort Collins High School.

I glanced over at Caitlin. She didn't look bored at all. Instead, she looked totally fascinated. Not a surprise. She spent her whole life watching football, talking about football, or playing football with the boys in the neighborhood. And she'd been going to every single Friday night game so far this year.

I looked back toward the field just as Iain hiked the ball. Milo ran out toward the goalposts, and the quarterback, Davis Jenkins, stepped back with the ball in his hand, looking for a receiver. Caitlin cupped her hands around her mouth and yelled, "He's open."

Milo jumped into the air, hands outstretched, and pulled in the football from an almost-impossible angle. Cait's dad shouted his approval, then blew a whistle to gather up the team.

I checked my phone. Still no text from Jameson. I'd seen him, briefly, at lunch—he'd come up to me in the cafeteria to say he had to practice with his band and we'd catch up later. He'd given me a quick kiss on the cheek, but things still felt . . . different.

Out on the field, Davis pulled off his helmet and jogged over to me and Caitlin. "What do you think?" he asked, sitting down beside Caitlin. He picked up a plastic squirt bottle and sprayed a stream of water into his mouth. Half of it splashed onto his face and he used the hem of his T-shirt to wipe it off, revealing a ripped stomach from hours of lifting weights in the off-season.

I knew he was waiting for Caitlin to pile on the compliments, but she was making him wait for it.

I filled in the silence between them. "Great throw."

Davis nodded at me, but his eyes still watched Cait.

"The offense looks good. You've got a lot of protection from your line," she finally said.

He frowned at her. "And?"

Cait closed her eyes for a beat, and I chewed awkwardly on the corner of my lip. Then Caitlin turned her head and opened her eyes to stare at Davis. "What can I say? The out route was on target. You put the ball right in Milo's hands when he cut to the sideline? This is definitely going to be your year and you are the accuracy master." She said it all in a monotone, but Davis's dark brown eyes lit up. Just like me, he knew Caitlin was the best judge of talent here today. And it didn't hurt that she might mention some of her opinions to the coach.

"Accuracy master. I like the sound of that," Davis said, and grinned like the sun had just popped out above the foothills. He lifted a hand and waved to the cheerleaders practicing on the track. Ben Kahale, Davis's boyfriend, waved back, then executed a perfect tumbling sequence ending in a backflip.

Davis cupped his hands around his mouth and yelled, "Show-off."

Davis and Ben were super sweet together. It made me think of Jameson *again*. Ugh. To distract myself, I glanced back at the practice. Eli Vernon kicked a field goal from the twenty-yard line. It was shaky, but it went through the goalposts. Barely.

"Oof," I said. Even *I* knew that wasn't great.

"He's getting better," Davis said.

Caitlin shook her head. "Not really."

"You're right," Davis said. "But he's all we have."

"I bet you could do that, Cait," I said, thinking of how amazing Caitlin was out on the soccer field. She made scoring goals look easy. "I mean, is kicking a soccer ball that different from kicking a football?"

Davis looked like I had just said something weird and magnificent at the same time. "Wait," he whispered. He turned to Caitlin. "Annie's right. Cait, you should be our kicker."

Caitlin rolled her eyes and made a face like it was the most ridiculous thing she'd ever heard. "Yeah. Sure. I'll do it," she muttered.

"Dare you." Davis's grin spread.

Caitlin shook her head. "Come on. A girl joining the football team?" she said. "I don't think my dad would go for it."

"You never know," I said.

Caitlin shrugged. "Well, all the guys would go ballistic. Especially Milo."

"Maybe he's not as bad as you think," Davis said.

"Come on," I said. "You're not a Milo fan, too, are you?"

"I'm withholding judgment," Davis said.

I looked at Caitlin, but she was staring out at the field with a fierceness I knew all too well.

"If you want something, Cait, you have to go for it," I told her. "The fact that there's never been a girl on the football team at Fort Collins High School just means it hasn't happened *yet*."

Cait looked thoughtful. She pulled out her phone, tapped at it for a few minutes, then showed the screen to me and Davis. She'd created a poll, but she hadn't posted it on ChitChat yet.

SHOULD A GIRL BE ALLOWED ON THE FOOTBALL TEAM?

- Yes
- No
- Undecided

Davis looked impressed. "I have to admit, Cait. You got guts," he said. "But if the odds are in your favor, you have to talk with your dad." He pulled his helmet on over his head and ran back out onto the field.

I glanced at Caitlin, then nodded down at her phone. "Are you really going to post that?"

She took a deep breath. "I think so. What do I have to lose?"

I watched as she hit post, and the poll went out into the world. Now we would wait to see what people said. ChitChat always had the answers.

CHAPTER THREE

What is it you plan to do with your one wild and precious life?

—Mary Oliver

At home, after dinner, I flopped onto my bed, scrolling through ChitChat and—okay, maybe—waiting for Jameson to text me.

I voted yes on Caitlin's poll, then checked the results. A lot of people had liked the post and commented, but not that many had voted yet. (There were five yeses and one no.) The poll would run for the rest of the week, though. I hoped Caitlin wasn't watching it obsessively. She probably was.

I stared up at the black-and-white poster of the Eiffel Tower on the ceiling above my bed. That image was always the last thing I saw before I closed my eyes at night and the first thing I saw when I woke up in the morning. It was iconic, classic, and everyone who went anywhere went to the Eiffel Tower.

Luna once told me that an average human spent six whole years dreaming. (It was one of those random facts she always seemed to have floating about in her brain from researching some story.) And yet, with all that dreaming I did every night, I never once dreamed of Paris when I slept. Only when I was fully awake.

I looked down at ChitChat again. I went to the page of one of my favorite travel accounts, and scrolled to a video of the *real* Eiffel Tower just as the sun set over Paris. The lights of the tower twinkled to life, illuminating the boats on the river below. My breathing slowed. Even if I never had the chance to see it in real life, it was here in my hand.

My finger pushed up on the screen to reveal a photo of a waterfall dropping off the cliffs on the Isle of Skye in Scotland. Next I scrolled down to a video of a dense jungle in Costa Rica. I turned up the sound to hear the roar of howler monkeys as they jumped from treetop to treetop. My mouth twitched into a smile. So many places waited for me with just a skimming touch of my finger. Next was a photo of a rooftop pool in Singapore. I imagined how the water might feel lapping at my manicured toes high above the multicolored lights of the glass-and-steel skyline.

I'd never been over the Colorado state line except when my father accidentally drove five miles into Kansas looking for a gas station. But one day, I hoped, I'd see the real-life version of the tiny houses set out on stilts over the turquoise-blue waters of Tahiti. The world was bigger than my room . . . my house . . . and my town.

Unfortunately, my family couldn't afford to take lavish trips, or really any trips at all. My mom was a nurse and my dad drove a Morningside Dairy delivery truck. It was all my parents could do to raise me and my sister. A Paris vacation, or any kind of vacation, wasn't a financial possibility. My dad worked. My mom worked. Then my dad worked again at the university as a parking attendant on football weekends.

There was a knock on my bedroom door.

"What?" I called, already knowing who was standing outside.

The door swung open, and my older sister, Savanna, came in carrying a stack of bridal magazines. Savanna and I looked the same, but different. She was taller and thinner, but we both had wavy blond hair and eyes the color of faded blue jeans. I think our eyes were what made people sometimes stop and turn around when they saw us. Savanna was comfortable with that. I was not.

"Can you look at these dresses?" Savanna asked. "I want to narrow down some options before we go shopping on Saturday. If not, we'll be there all day."

I did not want to spend my Saturday at a bridal shop, but I knew I had to be there for my sister. Savanna and Miguel had announced their engagement last month and the wedding plans were consuming every family conversation and activity. When Savanna transferred back home to Colorado her junior year of college last year, I thought we'd spend more time together. But of course she ended up spending almost all her time with her high school sweetheart, Miguel. And now they were getting *married*. The

wedding would be this summer, after they'd both gradu-
ated from college.

I liked Miguel and I was happy for Savanna, but sometimes I wanted to talk about something besides color
schemes and flower choices with her.

"Not now," I said. "I'm doing my homework."

"Doesn't look like it," Savanna said.

I made a big production of putting my phone down, sitting up, and reaching to grab my backpack off the floor.
I pulled out my geometry textbook and held it up to my
sister.

"See?" I said.

Savanna was peering at my phone where it lay faceup
on my bed. "Somebody's texting you," she said. "A lot."

It was probably Jameson. *Finally.*

"It's just something on ChitChat," I told her, then waved
her off toward the door, magazines and all. "Go on. I'll
look at your first choices later. Promise."

After Savanna left, I picked up my phone. Milo Moretti,
of all people, had posted a new video on ChitChat, and
tagged me in it, so I was getting all the notifications of likes
and comments. He'd used the hashtag #Annson. Why?

I pushed the black triangle on the middle of the screen
to bring the video to life.

The first thing I noticed was the unusual angle—almost
like the camera or phone was in someone's lap shooting
straight up. It was in the back seat of a car. Jameson's face

was clearly recognizable, his blond hair thick and curly. I always told him he spent more money on hair products than I did. It was a running joke between us, and it made me smile to think of it.

"Are you coming with us or not?" The question came from a voice off camera, but I recognized it as Milo's.

On the screen, Jameson shrugged and smiled. My heart melted a little like it always did when Jameson smiled. His familiar face filled the screen—square jaw, long nose, and beautiful golden-brown eyes that crinkled up just right when he laughed. I wanted to reach into the screen and brush away his hair from his eyes. Instead, I sat mesmerized and unmoving. Something wasn't right.

Milo's voice jerked me back to reality. "This is going to be an amazing party—and you're going to miss out because you have a *girlfriend*?"

My eyes widened in disbelief. I cringed at the tone in Milo's voice, and even though he was out of sight, I could imagine the sneer on his face when he asked, "Do you have to ask *permission*?"

Jameson frowned. He didn't look at the camera. It was as though he didn't even know it was there. "She doesn't tell me what to do," he said.

I realized I was holding my breath. He was talking about me. I knew it, but couldn't wrap my head around it. I leaned forward, my face almost touching the screen.

"Really? That's not what I hear." Milo was goading him, but Jameson wasn't going to take the bait.

My heart beat so loudly in my ears that it sounded like someone knocking incessantly on the door. *Say something,* I begged silently to the screen.

And then he did.

"Look, she's not going to be my girlfriend much longer. Okay?" Jameson said. "I just have to figure out how to tell her."

"Dude," Milo laughed. "I think you just did."

The screen went black and the comments poured in like tiny knives stabbing into an already open wound.

UH-OH. TROUBLE IN PARADISE. #ANNSON

WHAT A WAY TO FIND OUT! #ANNSON

OUCH! BREAK UP VIA CHITCHAT????? #ANNSON

???? SERIOUSLY. DID I JUST SEE THAT?

WHO CARES ABOUT ANNSON???? NO ONE!

HEY, HONEY. YOU CAN ONLY HIDE THOSE EXTRA POUNDS FOR SO LONG. EVERYBODY SEES THEM. EVEN YOUR BOYFRIEND OBV.

#ANNSON IS SOOOOOOOOOOOO DONE.

YA THINK?

WOW. CAN'T LOOK AWAY FROM THIS DUMPSTER FIRE.

I watched the video again. Then again. The comments piled up like land mines, the tiny red number on the notification button at the corner of my screen going up and up and up. My heart pounded, rapid and crazy. I couldn't move. A text pinged onto my screen.

LUNA: ARE YOU OKAY?

ME: NO

CAITLIN: HANG ON. WE'RE COMING OVER.

⏻   ⏻   ⏻

"Did you see it?" My voice was barely audible from the pile of pillows as I lay facedown on my bed. My friends stood silently in my room. "Of course you did. Everyone saw it."

How could I be the same person who just this morning strolled into school with a perfect boyfriend? In the few seconds of a ChitChat video, my whole life had changed.

I rolled over, brushing a hand over my face and smearing black mascara down one cheek. I looked at Caitlin and Luna, who were both still watching me, the pity plain on their faces. I felt the heaviness in the room.

"How could he do that to me?" I asked, my voice harsh.

Luna shook her head in response and sat down on the bed beside me. After a minute, Caitlin sat down on my other side.

Then I whispered, "And why?"

Luna looked like she was searching for an answer to my question. Any answer. But there wasn't one, and it was obvious by the look on her face. I glanced at Caitlin, who could only watch me with a small frown. It was going to be impossible to say the right thing. I knew it and they knew it.

Finally, Luna spoke. "It's going to be okay," she said, patting my knee.

"Don't say that," I snapped. "You don't know. Nobody knows the future, not even you."

Luna blinked, and I instantly felt terrible.

"I'm sorry," I said. "I know it's not your fault. I shouldn't take this out on you." I buried my face in my hands and let out a sob.

"I understand," Luna said softly.

Caitlin put her arm around me. "This is a lot to take in all at once. Give it some time," she pleaded. "Maybe it's not what it looks like."

"He was pretty clear. And so are all the ChitChat comments. Have you seen them?" I asked. I picked up my phone and glared at my screen. The comments were still pouring in, piling up. They were endless. And so cruel. "I can't stop reading them," I admitted.

Caitlin reached for my phone. "Don't read them. Don't wallow," she said in the voice her dad had used a thousand times to tell players to get back on the field and play their best whether they were losing or not.

"Shush," Luna said, stretching her hand across me to tap Caitlin on the arm. "It's her right to wallow."

I clutched the phone to my chest. My eyes still burned with tears, but I swallowed them down. "I just feel so . . ."

"Stupid?" Cait asked helpfully. I lifted my head and shot her a squinty-eye look.

"Ugly," I said quietly.

"You know there is nothing further from the truth," Luna said. "Remember when we first met, when we were little, and I thought you were a princess? Not the *Oh, I'm so helpless someone come and save me* kind of princess. More like the kind that mirrors said was *the most beautiful in the land.*"

I sniffed. "I remember," I whispered. Our childhood seemed so long ago.

"You're not ugly. Or stupid." Caitlin laid her head on my shoulder.

"Thanks," I told my friends.

But looking ugly and feeling ugly were two completely different things.

"Maybe you should talk to Jameson," Luna suggested. "Find out from him what's going on."

I knew she was right. I turned my phone over in my hand, ignored ChitChat for the time being, and texted Jameson:

ME: WE NEED TO TALK.

He didn't write back and I wondered if he would.

I looked at the home screen on my phone: a photo of me and Jameson, all dressed up for the Valentine's Day dance last year. In the photo, Jameson gazed adoringly at me, but I smiled straight into the camera. We looked like something out of *Teen Vogue*. That's how well we fit together. But that perfect facade was obviously a lie.

I didn't know what to do, but I was sick of looking at that photo, sick of waiting for Jameson to text me back, and sick of checking ChitChat. Before I could think, I hurled my phone across the room, where it lay facedown on the carpet against the far wall.

"Well, that's one way to solve the problem," Caitlin said dryly.

I swiped at my eyes. Even though it had felt good to throw the phone, part of me was worried I'd broken it. My parents would be furious, and likely would not get me a new phone anytime soon. I stood up and picked up the phone to make sure it was still working. It was, and now there was a text from Jameson waiting for me.

JAMESON: YEAH. LET'S MEET IN THE COURTYARD TOMORROW DURING LUNCH.

I swallowed hard. Jameson hadn't tried to apologize or explain. That meant that what I feared was coming true. This was the end of #Annson.

CAITLIN: MORNING, A. DID YOU GET SOME SLEEP?

ANNIE: BARELY. KEPT CHECKING CHITCHAT AND CRYING.

LUNA: I DECIDED. THE THREE OF US ARE GOING TO SCHOOL TOGETHER TODAY. I'M DRIVING.

ANNIE: THANKS. I THINK IT'S SAFE TO ASSUME JAMESON ISN'T PICKING ME UP.

CAITLIN: YOU'RE GONNA BE OKAY. YOU'RE GOING TO WALK INTO SCHOOL WITH YOUR HEAD HELD HIGH.

LUNA: AND WE'LL BE WITH YOU THE WHOLE TIME. XOXOXO

CHAPTER FOUR

It's sad, but sometimes moving on with the rest of your life starts with goodbye.

—Carrie Underwood

When Luna, Caitlin, and I used to play make-believe as kids, Caitlin was always the superhero who swooped in to battle the evil villains. And she always won the fight, because her legs were toned and muscled from kicking soccer balls and footballs and sometimes even kicking me or Luna—but only when we totally deserved it. And it was always just a tap.

But, I realized the next morning as I sat up in bed, Caitlin wasn't going to be able to save me now. Neither was Luna. I was grateful to be going to school with both of them. But I would still have to face my classmates on my own, no matter what.

I was exhausted after only a couple of hours of sleep. I had been looking at ChitChat on and off all night, but I couldn't resist looking again. I grabbed my phone off my nightstand, and there were new comments waiting for me.

THAT #ANNSON VIDEO WAS . . . SOMETHING

HA! EVEN THE PERFECT COUPLE ISN'T SO PERFECT #LOSER #ANNSON

SURE I FEEL SORRY FOR #ANNSON BUT STILL HERE FOR
THE DRAMA

DIDN'T SEE THAT ONE COMING!!! #ANNSON

WHAT SHE SAID #ANNSON

SERIOUSLY, #ANNSON. HAVE YOU SEEN YOURSELF????
ONE OF YOU IS NOT LIKE THE OTHER.

I read every single one of them. I couldn't stop. But
finally, knowing that Luna and Caitlin would be here
soon, I put down the phone and dragged myself out of
bed. My parents had left for work, and my sister had an
early morning class, so the house was empty, thankfully.

In the shower, no amount of hot water could wash
away the tears. I sobbed, my face turned up toward the
pouring water and my back heaving. There were no
conscious thoughts in my brain. Everything just hurt.
When the tears finally slowed, the feeling of emptiness
was still there. I sniffed, then turned off the water and
stood still for a few moments, my head resting against
the tiled wall. Finally, I took a deep breath and slid open the
bright yellow shower curtain, stepping out into the steamy
bathroom. I waited, dripping on the soft white rug.

"Okay," I whispered. "You can do this."

Steam covered the mirror, and I hesitated to wipe it off.
I wrapped myself in a thick buttery towel and stared at

my blurred image, willing life outside the bathroom door to be different when I opened it. Drips of water ran down the mirror, revealing only slivers of my face, until at last I reached out a hand and wiped the fog off completely. There I was. My outer shell looked exactly like it had yesterday, even though everything inside had completely changed.

⏻   ⏻   ⏻

Caitlin, Luna, and I walked into school with our arms tightly linked, which made me feel a lot better. But the minute the bell rang and we had to go our separate ways to class, I no longer had their protection.

The gauntlet stretched out in front of me like a dark jungle path with hiding leopards ready to rip out my throat with their sharp teeth.

It's just a hallway, I told myself. *Not a jungle.*

The combination of deep breaths and the way my heart pounded made me feel dizzy. I made myself walk ahead, toward math class. With my books clutched tight to my chest and my phone zipped securely inside my backpack, I tipped my face up slightly, chin jutted out.

Put one foot in front of the other.

Classmates were all around me, laughing and talking, but none of them had emojis bubbling up over their heads to let me know exactly what they were thinking.

I tried to freeze a smile on my face, but I knew I must look like some kind of weird creepy clown. It didn't matter what I looked like anyway. Not anymore.

I straightened my back and took two more steps.

"I think Jameson is adorable."

His name caught my attention. Even though I didn't want to look, I glanced quickly toward the voice.

Mariah Hadad.

Mariah and her best friend, Jordyn Hull, were lingering in the hall outside a classroom. Mariah was tall and slender, with legs impossibly too long for her body. She was gorgeous, with long, wavy black hair and big brown eyes, and her makeup was always perfect. She worked at the Macy's fragrance counter after school, so she was always wearing a new perfume. Today it was a mix of lavender and grapefruit.

Jordyn was just as thin, but petite. She was always laughing hysterically at everything Mariah and the other popular girls said.

"Are you *sure* he's really available?" Mariah asked, and Jordyn nodded enthusiastically. A thread of jealousy pulled tight at my stomach. I tried to breathe normally—in and out—without gasping for air. But my chest felt heavy, like it was full of sand.

Of all the people in the world, of course Mariah would be the one who would be interested in Jameson. She was always the one to comment on a ChitChat post if Jameson wore something new or cut his hair. In real life, whenever Jameson said something slightly amusing, Mariah would laugh and then Jordyn would join in like it was way funnier than it actually was.

"I'm positive. Have you seen this?" Jordyn held out her phone, and Mariah stared down at it. I knew what they were looking at. I didn't need to see it again. I made my feet keep moving toward the open classroom door.

Too late. Mariah suddenly glanced up and caught me watching. Her face twisted into an awkward smile. Jordyn glanced around the crowded hallway, then over at me. They both looked as though someone just caught them cheating on an exam.

I gritted my teeth, then gathered my strength and looked Mariah square in the face. "What's up?"

The question was chum thrown in the water between us. Mariah and I locked eyes, and I held her gaze, determined not to flinch.

"Not—not much," Mariah stammered, then recovered enough to smirk just a little. "You?"

"I'm great," I said, daring the two of them to say otherwise.

Then I turned and walked inside my math classroom, leaving them behind. I couldn't believe I'd done that. My arms were shaking. I wasn't fooled by this tiny victory, though. It was only the beginning and I needed to conserve all my energy to make it through the day.

I walked to my desk. All the faces around me blurred into noise, but I could see that most of my classmates had their phones out in their hands. I resisted the urge to check ChitChat and read more hateful comments.

I sat down, slumping behind Iain, who was, of course, on his phone. No doubt he'd seen the video, and probably "liked" it. My fingers clenched so tight under the desk that my hands cramped up into claws. I made myself stop, but then immediately began picking at an invisible thread on the leg of my jeans.

Don't check your phone. Don't check your phone.

I tried to focus on other things. The teacher's desk, with its pile of papers. The whiteboard behind the desk, with today's homework assignment in red at the top right under the date. I concentrated on those familiar things. The world had not ended overnight no matter how I felt this morning.

Ms. Garcia walked into the classroom, and her eyes scanned the room until they landed on me. She gave me a small smile of encouragement, and a few students swiveled around in their desks to stare. I realized that even the teachers knew what had happened last night on ChitChat. I sank a little lower in my desk.

Finally, I couldn't stand it any longer. I pulled out my phone and looked. My friends had texted me.

LUNA: WHAT'S WRONG WITH PEOPLE? THERE'S NO REASON FOR THAT KIND OF MEAN.

CAITLIN: I THINK YOU SHOULD REPORT THEM, A. DO YOU WANT ME TO DO IT?

LUNA: GIFS? CAT PICS? WHAT DO YOU NEED?

CAITLIN: MAYBE U NEED TO KICK SOMETHING?

A lump formed in my throat. It must be bad. I slid my phone farther under the desktop. My trembling finger hovered over the ChitChat icon; then I tapped it open. It was a mistake.

RABBIT FACE? OR FAT FACE????

CAN'T SAY I BLAME HIM FOR DUMPING HER. SHE'S REALLY LET HERSELF GO.

THE ONLY THING MORE ANNOYING THAN HER BODY IS HER FACE #ANNSON

ANNIE WEBB: HOT OR NOT? DEFINITELY NOT!!!!

My head filled with a sound like the roar of howler monkeys. The tide of comments turned against me, and there was nothing I could do to stop it. I blinked hard, then put my phone away in my bag.

The rest of the morning swirled around me. I couldn't think about science or history or literature. All I thought about was what I was going to say when I finally saw Jameson face-to-face. When the bell rang for lunch, I found him sitting on a bench in the courtyard. Just sitting there doing absolutely nothing. Not reading. Not playing a game on his phone. He looked down at his feet, biting the corner of his mouth. I knew that look. I'd seen it plenty of times. Like when he didn't want his dad to know he dented the car on the pole outside the Sonic Drive-In. Or when he was avoiding telling me he accidentally broke the red-heart-covered mug I gave him for Valentine's Day. But the heart he was breaking this time was mine.

I looked around the courtyard. Clusters of kids gathered on the sidelines, shooting furtive glances our way. A few even had phones out in their hands pointed in my direction. I intentionally tried to meet all their eyes—one by one—until eventually they lowered their cameras, if only for a few minutes. I knew ChitChat would still be full of videos and posts about my heartbreak. This was the biggest show in town.

I sat down beside Jameson. Suddenly I couldn't breathe. My throat closed. I could barely swallow.

"Hi," I finally said.

"Hi," Jameson replied. We were both silent for a while until Jameson spoke again.

"I didn't mean for you to find out like that." He pushed his sneaker into the rocks at his feet. He was still not looking me in the eye. "That video wasn't supposed to happen."

"How was it supposed to go?" I demanded. Jameson searched for something else to look at besides me. It only made me angrier. "How?"

Jameson shook his head. He rubbed his face with his hands and stumbled for an answer. "I don't know what to do. Milo posted it. He's the only one who can delete the video."

"Even if the video gets deleted, it doesn't matter," I snapped. "Everyone has already seen and shared it hundreds of times. There are no take-backs on the internet."

"I'm sorry," Jameson mumbled. "I shouldn't have . . . said those things."

"What are you saying? You were just joking around?" I knew in my heart that wasn't true, even though there was some tiny piece of me that would have believed him if he said it was.

Jameson didn't answer right away, which was all the answer I needed. "It's just . . ." he finally said. "I've been thinking about this stuff . . . for a while."

"Say it." My head hurt. I had this weird calm feeling and my voice was flat. Matter-of-fact. "I need to hear it from you, not from a ChitChat video."

Jameson tried to meet my eyes, but his glance skittered off again to the ground by my feet. "I want to break up," he said finally.

"So I heard," I said, my voice cracking.

He kept his gaze on the ground. "Things just aren't the same."

"You mean I don't *look* the same. That's why you're breaking up with me, isn't it?"

"It's not about how you look. It's not about you at all," Jameson said. I cringed at the stereotypical breakup line.

"Then why?" I hated the desperation in my voice, but I needed a reason.

I didn't get one. At least not one that made any sense. He shrugged. "I need some space to figure things out."

I didn't know what that meant. We figured things out together. That's what we did. "What things?"

"Just some stuff. About me." He stood up suddenly, pacing back and forth in front of the bench. "The band is really getting some attention. Now Milo wants to hang out. I feel like I could be part of something bigger."

I frowned. "And there's not room for me?"

"I know. I know," he said. "It sounds terrible."

"Yes, it does," I replied, feeling the tears start in my eyes. "It sounds like I'm not good enough for you." A sudden rush of heartache pounded through my body. "I was the biggest supporter of your band, remember?"

"I'm sorry," he said softly. The words struck like arrows.

"You're *sorry*?" My voice was too loud. Two boys walking by with tennis rackets stopped to stare. I felt like I was going to be sick. Jameson reached out to touch my shoulder, and I jerked away. "How long have you felt this way?"

He shrugged again and, after an awkward silence, put his hands in his pockets. "I don't know. For a while now. I just didn't want to hurt you."

"Well, I *am* hurt." More like destroyed. Shattered.

No reply. His shoulders dropped. "I never wanted that."

Jameson stopped pacing. The air suddenly felt cold. I shivered as though someone had touched the back of my neck.

"So, this is over?" I asked.

He finally looked in my eyes. His face. So familiar. His voice. I'd know it anywhere. I forced myself to hold his gaze.

"I think so," he said.

I crumpled in on myself, but I blinked hard to keep the tears from spilling out.

"Are you okay?" Jameson asked.

"What do you care?" Humiliation made my voice even sharper.

"Of course I care about you, Annie. That hasn't changed." He reached out to touch my shoulder again, but this time I stood up.

Despite my best efforts, the tears leaked out the edges of my eyes and down my cheeks. I knew people all around were watching. Before I could embarrass myself even more, I turned and hurried away. But I didn't go back into the school. I couldn't. I'd never cut class before, and I felt bad for doing it, but I would tell my teachers I'd been sick. I felt sick anyway.

I left the campus and started walking. Out of habit, I looked down at my phone and checked ChitChat. As I suspected, videos of my conversation with Jameson had already been posted, and there was a new hashtag: #AnNOson. I read the comments posted below each video.

DID I SERIOUSLY JUST WITNESS A BREAKUP IRL AND ON
CHITCHAT???

Y'ALL FAMOUS! #ANNOSON

YOU R AN IDIOT. GROW UP, GIRL. HE'S DONE #ANNOSON

UR DEFINITELY SINGLE NOW #ANNOSON

I kept walking, and walking, and realized I was walking home. It would take forever, but I didn't care.

As long as I didn't have to go back to school.

LUNA: OH MY GOD ANNIE I SAW THE NEW VIDEO. I'M SO SORRY WHERE ARE YOU???

CAITLIN: WE'RE IN THE CAFETERIA. SOMEONE SAID THEY SAW YOU LEAVE SCHOOL?

LUNA: ANNIE????

CHAPTER FIVE

*I gave him my heart, and he took it and pinched it to death; and
flung it back to me.*

—Emily Brontë, *Wuthering Heights*

"You could have texted us sooner. We were freaking out,"
Luna said when I opened the door to find her and Caitlin
on my doorstep after school. I'd finally texted them back
once I got home, to let them know I was alive.

"Seriously," Caitlin said, looking worried. "Don't disappear on us again, okay?"

"I know. I'm sorry," I said, walking back into the living room and collapsing on the couch. My phone lay silent
and dark on the dining room table. I'd turned it off after
texting my friends, and then I'd spent the rest of the afternoon mindlessly flipping channels between reality shows
and *Judge Judy* just to try to keep from thinking about
Jameson and ChitChat.

Luna and Caitlin joined me on the couch. Luna put her
arm around me.

I immediately felt my eyes welling up again. "I feel
horrible."

"What hurts?" Luna asked. I rested my head on her
shoulder.

Sniffling, I whispered, "My heart."

"Jameson is an idiot," Caitlin declared. "And so is everybody else on ChitChat."

I lifted my head from Luna's shoulder. "Not everybody," I argued, sort of pointlessly.

Caitlin was looking at her phone, and she let out a huff. "Have you seen what people are commenting on my poll?"

"No," I admitted. I'd been so wrapped up in my own drama I'd forgotten about Caitlin's poll.

Caitlin shook her head. "The no votes are climbing. People in the comments are saying I *could* be on the football team if I weren't the coach's daughter. They're saying it's about nepotism, not talent." She frowned.

"Ignore them," Luna said. "I voted yes, of course."

"So did I," I chimed in, wiping my eyes.

"Thanks," Caitlin said. "But those other voices are not so easy to ignore." She glanced at me sympathetically. "Right?"

I nodded, then burst into fresh tears as my friends sat beside me in silence.

"I'm sorry that you guys have to keep seeing me like this," I sobbed. "But I think I know what I need to do." It had come to me while I was watching TV. "I think I need a break. A new start." My voice grew stronger with each word.

"What do you mean?" Caitlin asked.

"I'm not going back to school," I said firmly. "Not tomorrow. Not ever."

"Of course you're going back to scho[

"Where else would you go?"

"I'll transfer to Rocky." Rocky Mou[

was the rival school across town.

Caitlin stood up with her hands on her hips. "No way.

You're not changing schools because of some . . . boy."

"It's not just because of Jameson," I argued, feeling a

pang at even saying his name. "It's what *everyone* at school

is saying. You should have seen how Mariah looked at me

today." I shuddered. "I walked by her just as she was ask-

ing Jordyn if Jameson was really available."

"Ugh." Luna rolled her eyes.

"Mariah and Jordyn are the worst," Caitlin chimed in.

"But it's even worse on there." I nodded to my phone.

Luna sighed. "I know it's really hard right now. But come

on, Annie. You can't transfer schools. You can't leave us."

I knew what she meant. The thought of going to

school—any school—without my two best friends was ter-

rifying. This year was supposed to be our best year ever.

I tried to reassure all of us. "I'll still have you guys, but

we just won't see each other every day at school."

Caitlin wasn't having any of it. She shook her head

vehemently. "You're not going anywhere. We're in this

together."

"Besides," Luna added, "I'm sure there are just as many

jerks at Rocky as there are at our school."

That was probably true. There were mean kids every-

where. And then a new, awful thought took hold as I

stared at my phone. Who was to say all the rude comments stopped at the doors of my high school? Some kids at Rocky might have already seen the posts. And anyone I met there would be able to find out everything about me within seconds. Especially if they knew the right hashtag.

"You're right. It doesn't matter," I said bleakly. "I can't run away even if I wanted to. I wouldn't escape ChitChat even if I went to a new school."

Luna frowned. "What if we blocked and reported everyone who was posting horrible things?" she suggested. "ChitChat must have some rules about cyberbullying." She pulled her phone out of her pocket. "I'll start doing it now."

"Same," Caitlin said, sitting back down with her phone.

"Thanks, guys, but it's pointless," I said, watching them and feeling empty. "We don't know if ChitChat can actually take any of those comments down. And people can just come up with new, creative ways to post mean stuff."

"What if we told a teacher about it?" Luna said, always looking for answers. She glanced at Caitlin. "Cait, you could ask your dad, right?"

"The teachers already know, I think," I cut in, remembering Ms. Garcia's sympathetic look today. "There's nothing they can do." I sighed. "There's nothing *we* can do."

"But we *can* do something," Caitlin said, her brow furrowed. She looked carefully from me to Luna. "We can turn it off."

I frowned at her. "Turn off *what* exactly? Our phones?" I picked up my blank phone. Shutting it off this afternoon *had* made me feel a little better, but I knew ChitChat was still out there, waiting.

"No," Caitlin said. "We turn off *ChitChat*. We deactivate our accounts. We delete it from our phones. We go offline."

I felt tiny bumps rise on my arm. It was such a simple idea. My life was so intertwined with ChitChat that I hadn't even considered I could just . . . leave it.

"Wait, yes!" Luna said, leaning forward, her eyes sparkling. "I recently read a news story about this. There are these, like, summer camps where adults and sometimes teens go and totally unplug from everything. They turn in their devices and aren't allowed to go online at all. Supposedly it helps them feel refreshed and happier."

"How long do they go offline?" Caitlin asked Luna, sounding intrigued.

"It depends," Luna said. "A few weeks? A month?"

"We can't give up our phones for *a month*," I said, gripping mine as if Luna was about to snatch it away. "What about texting? And email?"

"And phone calls," Caitlin chimed in. "Plus, I don't know about you guys, but my dad always has me text him if I go anywhere alone, to let him know I got there safely."

"Same with my parents," I said, and Luna nodded. That was an undeniable fact of our lives. "And we can't give up the internet," I added. "We need to research stuff for homework."

"And for news stories," Luna put in with a sigh.

We sat in silence for a moment, all looking down at our phones in our hands.

"Well, maybe it doesn't have to be that extreme," Caitlin spoke up. "The issue here is ChitChat, right? Social media?" She glanced between me and Luna. "We love it, but we kind of hate it, too." She talked fast, gathering steam as her idea took shape. "Maybe we deactivate all our social media accounts, and delete them from our phones and computers. And we don't go back on them. For . . . one month."

"No social media for a month?" The thought made my stomach tighten. "Then how do we document the important things in our lives?"

"We experience them," Caitlin answered with a shrug. "In real time."

"How does anyone know we actually did them, then?" I whispered.

"We know it," Caitlin said.

It still sounded extreme. I turned my phone back on and watched it glow to life in my hand. I felt a rising panic at the thought of disconnecting from everyone and everything. Not knowing what Jameson was doing, what he was posting. Not being able to follow my travel accounts. All those photos and videos . . . gone. My hand trembled.

But suddenly, the ChitChat notifications started pinging again in my hand. Three . . . eight . . . twenty-two . . . and climbing. I felt like throwing up. Maybe Caitlin was right. Maybe this was the only way. But . . .

"What about your poll?" I asked Caitlin. "Don't you want to see the results?"

Hesitation flashed across Caitlin's face. Of course she wanted to see what happened with her poll. Who wouldn't?

I turned to Luna. "And what if you need to be on social media for the paper?" I said.

My friends were both quiet, thinking.

"What if I just delete *my* apps?" I suggested. "I'm the one with the problem. You guys don't need to do it, too."

"No," Caitlin said. She glanced at her phone again, then looked back up at us. "The poll is stressing me out anyway. I can ask Davis or someone to tell me when the final results go up."

"And honestly, going off social media will probably help be me more productive with my writing," Luna said. She turned to me. "If you do it, we do it, Annie. That's how this works. We're in this together, like Cait said."

My heart melted and I blinked back tears. "Thank you, guys," I said, touched that they'd do all this for me. "But I don't know if I'll be strong enough to *really* stay off ChitChat," I admitted. "How can we resist the temptation? What's to stop us from just reactivating our accounts anytime we want?"

Luna bit her lip. "We should have rules," she said. Of

course she would say that. Luna was always the one to make up or enforce the rules.

"Like what?" Caitlin asked.

"Maybe we *limit* our time on our phones so we're not tempted," Luna explained. "For instance, I'm constantly texting you guys and checking my phone to see if I have new texts. Maybe we only text each other . . . what? Twice a day?"

My heart dropped, and Caitlin and I exchanged shocked glances. *Twice a day?* That was nothing. "Three times a day?" I offered.

"Fine," Luna said. She pulled out a notebook and pen from her backpack and turned to a fresh page. "We only text each other three times a day—unless there's an emergency, of course," she began, writing everything down in her notebook.

"I've got another rule," Caitlin said. "Maybe we say no screens after ten o'clock at night. I'm always cranky because I don't get enough sleep."

"Same," I admitted. I was often up too late scrolling on ChitChat or doing online shopping. "And maybe . . . no phones during breakfast, lunch, or dinner," I suggested. I thought about how my parents were always telling me to stop bringing my phone to the table.

"No phones while eating, no phones after ten," Luna repeated, scribbling away.

"And maybe we have some . . . reward," Caitlin said. "For staying offline."

Luna smiled. "Like what? Chocolate?"

"That's your answer to everything," I said.

Luna nodded. "Pretty much."

"No," I said, feeling a new strength in me. "Our reward is that we'll be free of ChitChat, and what everyone is doing and saying on there." I sat up straight and held up my phone. "Right?"

Luna reached out and grabbed my hand. "You're right." She looked at Caitlin. "Okay. Ready?"

Caitlin nodded.

I nodded, too, even though I didn't feel at all ready. I took a deep breath.

I watched as Luna pulled up her ChitChat account and hit DEACTIVATE. Then she pressed her finger to the ChitChat icon on her phone. A blue X appeared, and Luna clicked it.

"I just took ChitChat off my phone. There. Gone," she announced. Then she deactivated and deleted the rest of her social media apps.

"I'll go next," I said. It was the least I could do since Luna and Caitlin were making this sacrifice for me. I deactivated my ChitChat account, then pushed down tight on the ChitChat icon. It began to pulse with life and my finger hovered over the blue X when it appeared.

"Here goes nothing?" I looked up at the two faces staring at me. They nodded and I hit the delete button. Gone.

I thought I should feel better. Like a weight had been lifted from my mind. But honestly, I just felt nervous. Like something was missing. I pushed the feeling away and quickly deactivated and deleted my other social media apps. Then I looked up from the screen. "That's all of them. Now you," I said to Caitlin.

Caitlin deactivated and deleted all her social media apps, too. Then we sat in silence.

"Now we promise. No, something even more serious . . ." Caitlin snapped her fingers. "A . . . *vow*."

Luna and I exchanged a glance. We knew what Caitlin meant.

"Fire ring," I said solemnly, and Luna nodded. I looked at them both, wide-eyed. This was serious.

The first fire ring was when Caitlin's parents took us all camping the summer before middle school. Cait's mom was still alive then, and I remembered how we'd arrived at the campsite around dinnertime. The river was steps away, gurgling over the rocks and splashing into foam. Cait's mom spread out hot dogs, buns, chips, and all the fixings on the concrete picnic table while her dad set up the tent. Caitlin coached me and Luna on how to find sticks just the perfect length for cooking hot dogs over the fire. Later, after the adults were asleep and the hot dogs were long gone, the three of us sat around the fire talking about the scary prospect of going to middle school.

"Nothing will change," Caitlin said.

"Don't be silly. Things will change," I said quietly. "*We'll* change."

The flickers of the dying fire lit Luna's solemn face. "But we'll still be best friends."

Caitlin nodded. "Of course."

"Promise," I said.

I stretched my hands out to each side, and we leaned in to close the circle, our fingers entwining tightly. With the fire glowing in the middle, I said it first, then squeezed Luna's hand to pass it along.

"As this fire is my witness, I vow to always stay friends. No matter what. No matter how."

There were more fire rings after that, mostly at the outdoor firepit in Caitlin's backyard when the weather permitted. The ceremony was only to commemorate the most important things. Like when Luna decided to ask out Blake Place in seventh grade. And then when Caitlin's mom started losing her hair from cancer and Cait needed to help her shave the rest of it off.

And today, it seemed, was another big moment.

"Should we go to my backyard?" Caitlin offered.

I shook my head. I was worried I'd lose my nerve and rethink everything if we didn't take the vow right here and now.

"Get a candle," Luna said, reading my mind. "We'll have to make do."

I slid off the couch and went into the kitchen. After rummaging around in one of the drawers, I finally pulled out a pink glittery candle decorated with butterflies. I brought it back out to the living room and shrugged.

Caitlin laughed. "Seriously?"

"My grandmother gave it to me for Christmas."

"It's fine," Luna said, getting up from the couch. Caitlin stood, too.

The three of us settled onto the living room floor, our knees touching. I lit the candle and carefully placed it in the middle of the circle. We all stared at the flame.

"What do we say?" Luna asked.

"Simple." Caitlin crossed her arms. "We vow to stay off social media for a month."

We went around the circle and repeated the words: "As this fire is my witness, I vow to stay off social media for a month."

It sounded a little silly, but by the time we were done, the vow felt real.

"I bet we're the only three people in the whole school who aren't on social media," Caitlin finally said after a moment.

"Well," Luna said with a smile, "at least we're . . . unique."

I laughed and thought that no matter how hard this vow turned out to be, the laughter with my friends would help.

"What do we call ourselves?" Caitlin asked.

I frowned. "Do we have to have a special name?"

Caitlin nodded her head vigorously. "Absolutely. Team name."

"Okay," I said, thinking. "How about Team SO? Team Stay Offline?"

"That works," Caitlin said.

"Nice and simple," Luna agreed. She grabbed her

notebook off the couch and flipped to a new page. "And now we put it all in writing."

I vow <u>for one month</u> to . . .
★ Stay off all social media.
★ Not go online after ten p.m.
★ Not go online during breakfast, lunch, or dinner
★ Limit texting to three times a day

Signed: Team SO
Luna Ortega
Caitlin Stone
Annie Webb

CHAPTER SIX

I cannot give you the formula for success, but I can give you the
formula for failure, which is: Try to please everybody.

—Herbert Bayard Swope

As soon as I woke up the next morning, I reached for my phone. It was pure habit. Every morning, I had to check ChitChat for the latest posts. Then I'd text my friends. Then I'd check ChitChat again.

But this morning, my hand felt only empty space on my nightstand.

Then I remembered Jameson breaking up with me.

And the awful comments.

And the vow.

I also remembered how, before going to bed last night, I'd asked my sister if she could keep my phone in her room and not give it back to me until the morning. Thankfully, she hadn't asked any questions. That had been the only way I'd been able to go to sleep without feeling tempted to check my phone and download all the apps again. It would only take a few swipes and clicks to break the vow.

I sat up in bed. I felt weird and empty, like I was missing everything. Well, I sort of was.

When I went downstairs, Savanna was at the kitchen table eating a waffle for breakfast. I didn't always see her in the mornings, but I was up earlier than usual. She was flipping through a bridal magazine as she ate, and she had her phone and my phone on the table beside her.

"Here's your phone." Savanna held it out to me, and I took it carefully, like it might come to life with fangs that would latch on to my hand with teeth deep enough to scar.

"Is it broken?" Savanna asked me.

"W-what? No . . ." I stammered.

Her eyes narrowed. "Why did you give it to me last night?"

"I didn't want it waking me up." It was a lame excuse, but I wasn't ready to talk to Savanna about Jameson or ChitChat or the vow.

Savanna laughed. "You do know where the off switch is, right?"

"Ha, ha," I mumbled.

"What's up with you anyway?" Savanna asked. "You look depressed. You know nothing is changing with this wedding, right? I'm still going to be around; you just get a new brother."

I sighed. "It's not about the wedding. Or Miguel. It's just . . . things are different."

Savanna looked at me, then smiled sadly. "Yeah, change is hard. Even when it's a good change."

I wanted desperately to tell her all about everything and let her tell me exactly what to do. Like when she taught me how to ride a bike or when she showed me how to curl my hair without burning my fingers on the iron. But I knew

Savanna wasn't able to talk me through this one unless I was ready to share. And I wasn't.

I checked my phone to see if I had new texts from Caitlin and Luna. I knew we weren't supposed to text during breakfast time, but technically I wasn't eating yet.

> LUNA: THIS IS SO MUCH HARDER THAN I THOUGHT IT WOULD BE.

> CAITLIN: I KNOW. I KEEP THINKING ABOUT THAT POLL.

> LUNA: I ALMOST PUT CHITCHAT BACK ON MY PHONE THIS MORNING BUT STOPPED MYSELF.

> CAITLIN: GOOD. WE NEED TO STAY STRONG.

I fired off a text of my own.

> ME: I GAVE MY PHONE TO SAVANNA LAST NIGHT, BUT I CAN'T DO THAT EVERY NIGHT. I DON'T KNOW HOW I'M GONNA GET THROUGH THIS.

My mom came into the kitchen then, still in her nursing scrubs from the hospital, and opened the fridge. Since she worked the overnight shift in labor and delivery, it was dinnertime for her.

"Morning, girls," she said to me and Savanna.

I forced a smile and tried to forget about my phone for the moment.

"Any new babies?" I asked Mom.

"Not last night," she said, pulling out the leftover spaghetti and scooping it into a smaller bowl for the microwave. She punched a few buttons, then waited, yawning. I noticed how tired she looked. Working night shifts meant more money, and that was important with all the wedding expenses. Dad, meanwhile, had taken on extra shifts making deliveries with his truck. He was still out on the road this morning.

As I stood in the kitchen with my mom and my sister, I wanted to tell *both* of them what had happened—with Jameson, with ChitChat, with the vow. But before I could bring myself to speak, Mom turned to Savanna with a smile.

"I was thinking you'd look great in a ball gown," Mom said, nodding toward the bridal magazine in Savanna's hand. "Instead of a mermaid silhouette. What do you think?"

Savanna shrugged. "No promises until I actually try them on, but I just don't think the whole princess look is for me."

The microwave dinged, and my mom took out the bowl, frowning. "Just keep an open mind," she told my sister. I could tell she was rooting for a ball gown and that this whole dress thing was going to quickly become all kinds of family drama. My mom took her dinner out to the living room sofa and clicked on the television to watch the morning news.

I blinked, refocusing on the screen in my hand.

CAITLIN: WE'LL GET THROUGH IT TOGETHER. LEAVING FOR SCHOOL NOW WITH MY DAD. SEE YOU BOTH THERE?

LUNA: I HAVE ANOTHER NEWSPAPER MEETING BUT YES I'LL SEE YOU BOTH SOON. XOXOX

I took a deep breath. Right. School. This was not going to be easy at all.

⏻　⏻　⏻

Since Savanna didn't need the car that morning, I drove myself to school. I steeled myself as I walked inside the building. Unfortunately, the first person I saw was Jameson. He was walking down the hall with Santos Medina, the drummer for Discord, and they were both laughing like it was the best day in the world. My face burned. I tugged on my backpack straps and turned, heading the opposite way down the hall. Heads swiveled in my direction. I heard whispers and giggles.

My head felt like it might float off my shoulders, but

not in a good way. Not in the way it felt when Jameson would kiss me. Quickly, I blinked away the memory flash.

It didn't matter that I wasn't on ChitChat. The comments still scrolled through my brain.

SO SAD. THE CUTE COUPLE IS HISTORY.

FILTERS AIN'T GOING TO FIX YOU, BABE!

HAHAHA. EVERYONE FEELS SORRY FOR HER.

It was almost enough to make me want to pull out my phone and reinstall ChitChat. Just so I could see the comments again for myself, and respond to each and every one of them, in the cruelest way possible.

But I remembered the fire ring, and our signatures in Luna's notebook.

No ChitChat. Keep the vow.

⏻　⏻　⏻

As usual, the cafeteria at lunchtime was full of noise. I sat down at our regular table with my tray and glanced around the crowded room. Jameson must have been rehearsing with Discord, which was a relief—I didn't want to see him again. Luna and Caitlin weren't here yet, so my only option was to sit there looking completely lame. Every second, every minute, I felt the pull to seek ChitChat's escape from the real world.

I looked around the room one more time, but no one was looking at me. They weren't looking at anything except the screens in their hands. Hundreds of heads bowed over phones, holding a phone in one hand and a sandwich or a burrito in the other. Sometimes they glanced up to talk to a person across the table, but it was only a sentence or two before attention was back on the screens. Once or twice, as I watched, kids shoved screens across the table to show their friends something and I heard snippets of music or canned laughter. I realized suddenly that many of the people in this room were invisible, participating remotely through the tiny rectangles in every kid's hand. For a minute, I imagined all the virtual people standing at the shoulders of the real people—celebrities, friends, influencers—leaning over and whispering in ears. All of them talking at the same time, with different agendas.

I still wanted to pull my phone out of my backpack. It was like an invisible string connected my hand to the screen. What was I supposed to do? Just sit here and stare into space? My fingers started to slide under the table toward the backpack.

Luna plopped down in front of me with her tray just in time, and I jerked my hand back on top of the table. I didn't meet her eyes.

"How are you doing?" she asked. We hadn't seen each other since we'd met up at our lockers after homeroom.

"Just great," I said sarcastically. "You caught me almost reaching for my phone so I could put ChitChat back on."

"But you didn't!" she said, always looking for the positive. "The vow is working."

"Barely," I said. I happened to glance across the cafeteria then and caught sight of Mariah sitting with Jordyn and their popular friends. Mariah smirked at me and I looked away. "Why can't we delete people out of our lives as easily as our apps?" I asked, thinking that deleting the apps was already tough enough. "Like Mariah," I whispered. "She's staring at me."

"What's up, Team SO?" Caitlin joined us at the table with a tray of cafeteria pizza and French fries. She slammed the tray down so hard that French fries scattered across the tabletop.

I wrinkled my nose. "How can you eat that stuff?"

Caitlin took a big bite of the pizza, exaggerating her chewing. "It's delicious."

"Seriously, ignore Mariah," Luna said.

Caitlin nodded, taking another big bite. "That's always good advice," she mumbled with her mouth full.

I chewed on my bottom lip and met Luna's eyes across the table. "I need to check out what she's posting online."

Luna put her hand across the table to hold my arm down. "No, you don't."

I was disappointed, but I picked up my spoon and took a tiny bite of cottage cheese.

Luna distractedly took a French fry from Caitlin's tray and bit into it without realizing how hot it was. She instantly spit it out and blew on the remaining piece in her hand.

Caitlin frowned, putting down the pizza. She shot Luna a look. "I have to be honest. I'm having a harder time being on Team SO than I thought I would."

"I know. But, you guys, this is only day one!" Luna said. "We have a whole month to go."

"I really need to see everything people are saying about the poll, but now I can't even look to see how the votes are going," Caitlin said.

"I heard Davis talking about it before English class today," I admitted.

"And?" Caitlin asked.

I seriously wished I had better news, but I said, "Some of the guys have doubts."

Caitlin stiffened, then scrambled for her bag. "I can convince them!"

"Cait," Luna said sternly, then waited until Caitlin's eyes focused on her. "We took a vow. You know what that means."

Caitlin's hand dropped limply onto the plate next to her pizza.

"So, if we're not on ChitChat, what are we supposed to do instead?" I asked. "My brain is bouncing off the walls. I don't know what to do with my *hands*." I pushed my fingers through my hair. "I'm addicted. I admit it. I need my social media fix."

"Same," Caitlin said.

"Same," Luna admitted with a sigh.

Caitlin took another bite of pizza. We all looked at each other and listened to the background roar of cafeteria noise.

Finally, Luna shrugged. "People did stuff before they had social media, right?"

"Obviously," I said.

Silence again. Nobody had any easy answers.

"Let's meet after school today," Luna declared. "We'll figure out how we can get through this. "

I nodded decisively, and so did Caitlin.

"Let's meet in my backyard," Caitlin said. "No phones."

○　○　○

Leaving my phone behind on my desk that afternoon felt strange, but I forced myself to walk out the back door empty-handed. Outside, the blackbirds shrieked at one another in the top of the ash tree and the tiny wrens battled with a flurry of wings over the bird seed in the feeder.

I'd never really noticed the sounds of the birds before. Happy chirps. Angry screeches. It was like a whole conversation was going on outside in the backyard that I hadn't heard.

Even colors seemed more noticeable. I liked green. It was a good color. Usually not my favorite, but today it was hard to ignore. The sun turned the leaves of the Chinese plum tree lime green, while the other side of the tree stayed an almost black-green in the shadow. The firs on either side of the path were bushy and changed a shade darker, then lighter again, every time the wind blew slightly. Behind the pine, where the squirrels chased one another up and down, the aspen's bright green tips turned yellow, but soon would be red, orange, and, yes, still green.

It had only been about twenty-four hours since I removed ChitChat from my phone. It might not be a Costa Rican jungle or a Parisian garden, but I realized there might be something to see in my own backyard.

I climbed over the waist-high wooden slats of the fence and into Cait's backyard. It was a familiar way of entering and exiting. All our backyards lined a small open field with a dirt trail through the middle that led down to a lake.

Caitlin was sitting on one of the Adirondack chairs in her yard, a book open in her lap and a scowl on her face. It was too warm to have a fire going in the firepit.

"What are you doing?" I asked her as I approached.

Caitlin slammed the book closed. "Shakespeare. Test tomorrow."

"How's it going?"

"Not great." Cait shook her head, and I slumped into the Adirondack chair beside her. A squirrel ran down the fence, hopped onto the grass, then scurried up a pine tree. We both watched it like it was the most fascinating thing in the world. Normally, we would be checking our phones.

I closed my eyes, trying to enjoy the feel of the hot sun on my face. It almost felt like summer. But remembering the summer brought up flashes of Jameson and the time we spent together at the lake.

Whispers.

Kisses.

Laughter.

I opened my eyes, willing myself back to the present. Summer was gone and so was Jameson. I had to get used to it somehow.

Luna appeared and plopped down in the remaining chair. She had her trusty notebook with her, plus a stack of dusty-looking books I'd never seen before.

"Okay," she told us. "I did some research. And I went old-school. I got these books at the library."

Caitlin groaned. Luna thought research was the best thing ever about being a reporter. She loved following a lead deeper and deeper, every answer leading to another question. She said it was like an open-ended adventure that led to new plot twists, shocking facts, and bizarre details. But most of all, it allowed Luna to become an expert on anything and everything. Which was sometimes helpful, but sometimes annoying, like when she spouted random facts in the middle of a conversation.

In this case, though, I had a feeling her talent for research was going to be very helpful.

"Stop," I told Caitlin. "Let's see what she found."

"Thank you," Luna told me pointedly. She opened one of the library books, and then looked at both me and Caitlin. "We need to calm our monkey minds."

"What?" Caitlin said.

"Monkey mind is a Buddhist term meaning unsettled, restless, or confused," Luna explained patiently.

I snapped my fingers. "Yes. I saw a video of howler monkeys. That's exactly how my brain feels. Jumping around from thing to thing. And screaming. Always screaming."

Luna nodded like she completely understood. "So, if you let your mind race around and present it with too much stimulus at once, then you will never feel focused or at peace."

"I have to say, that makes sense," Caitlin said.

I scooted my chair closer to Luna's and peeked into her book. "Where do we start to calm down these monkeys? It's a bit overwhelming."

"We should find a how-to video on ChitChat," Caitlin suggested, then covered her mouth with her hand. "Oops. Sorry."

"We definitely need help," I said.

"Well," Luna said, flipping to a new page in the book. "Luckily, we have some answers in here." She paused triumphantly. "We can meditate."

Cait looked skeptical. "And exactly how do we do that?"

"'Find a comfortable seat,'" Luna read aloud.

"These are comfy." I leaned back against the chair, put my feet up on the firepit.

"True," Caitlin agreed.

"Okay, good," Luna said. "Now close your eyes."

I watched Cait shut her eyes. I closed mine, too, then opened one eye to peek at Luna. Her eyes were still open, because she was looking into her book.

"How are you supposed to do this with us if you are reading to us?" I asked her.

Luna frowned. "You go through it first; then we'll try it together."

"Fine." I placed my hands limply on my thighs, palms up. I touched my middle fingers to my thumbs to make a circle. With my eyes squeezed tight, I said, "I saw this wellness influencer meditating on ChitChat once. You're supposed to sit like this."

"Why?"

I opened my eyes and saw Cait now had one eye open.

"I don't know, but it can't hurt," I said sharply. My patience was giving out. Wasn't meditation supposed to make you calmer? Oops. I shut my eyes again. "What's next?"

"Take some deep, cleansing breaths," Luna instructed. "When you focus on your breathing, it helps keep your mind from wandering."

Cait panted like a dog outside on a sunny day.

"Not like that," Luna said. "Breathe in for six counts, then out for six counts. Slowly."

Luna counted and we breathed. I did feel a bit more relaxed than I had a few minutes ago.

"Now what?" I asked.

"'Clear your mind of everything,'" Luna read.

"But how do you do that?" Caitlin asked. "If you're

thinking about clearing your mind, then your mind is full of something."

My mind wasn't clearing either. I opened my eyes.

"You should try to sit still for a minute and think about what calms you," Luna said, and closed her book. "I'll do it with you."

We all three sat silently, breathing and trying not to think about not thinking.

Finally, Caitlin whispered, "So, we're doing it now, right?"

"I think so," I fake-whispered back.

"Shhh," Luna said.

"What are you thinking about?" Caitlin whispered.

"What Jameson is posting on ChitChat now," I said. "You?"

"The results of the poll," Caitlin whispered back.

"Shh," Luna whispered again. But then she added, "If Tamar has posted anything on ChitChat about the newspaper."

I opened my eyes. Both girls were staring back at me.

"I don't think we did it right," I said.

Luna sighed. "Okay," she said, opening another book. "One suggestion is to think of a favorite childhood memory." She glanced from me to Caitlin. "Maybe we can all think of something fun we did together?"

"Ohhhh," Caitlin said. "I like that one."

"Ice cream," I said decisively. "Ben and Jerry's on the square."

Luna and Caitlin grinned, and I knew they were remembering that day, too. We were eleven years old, and our parents had let us go to Ben & Jerry's on our own for the first time. We sat beside the fountain on the bench with our treats. I'd gotten a hot fudge sundae with whipped cream and sprinkles. Luna got a strawberry cone, and Caitlin, a large cup of Chunky Monkey. I closed my eyes and remembered the taste of the ice cream, the gooey amazingness. Kids were running around, and a guy was playing a jazzy song on the outdoor piano. The air was warm, and Caitlin was laughing because Luna's cone was melting faster than she could eat it.

I realized that the memory had finally taken my thoughts off ChitChat and Jameson. I opened my eyes and smiled at my friends. They looked calmer, too.

I felt a hopeful charge in the air. Maybe we *could* do this. We didn't have to follow the crowd into the endless posts and reposts. It felt like a new beginning. Or a small miracle.

CAITLIN: OOOOMMMMMM.
OOOOOOOMMMMM.

ANNIE: WHAT IS THAT SUPPOSED TO BE?

CAITLIN: SHHH. I'M MEDITATING.

LUNA: YEAH, RIGHT.

CAITLIN: WELL, I'M TRYING.

LUNA: POINTS FOR TRYING.

ANNIE: SO . . . HOW ARE WE ALL DOING,
THREE DAYS IN? #TEAMSO

LUNA: NOT GONNA LIE, I KEEP PICKING UP
MY PHONE TO CHECK CHITCHAT AND THEN
REMEMBERING.

ANNIE: LITERALLY SAME. ☹

CAITLIN: I'M DYING TO KNOW HOW THE
POLL IS GOING!!!!

LUNA: WE HAVE TO RESIST THE URGE TO
CHECK!

ANNIE: YES! WE CAN DO THIS!

LUNA: IT'S ALMOST TEN P.M. SCREENS
DOWN, REMEMBER?

ANNIE: *GRUMBLE* OK

CAITLIN: I CAN'T HEAR YOU. I'M
MEDITATING AGAIN.

CHAPTER SEVEN

It's not whether you get knocked down, it's whether you get up.

—Vince Lombardi

Once I saw a video of a sloth crossing the road while cars buzzed by on either side. That was sort of how I felt without ChitChat—meticulously crawling across the days while trying not to be crushed by everything whirling around me. The only difference was, people thought the sloth was adorable.

Staying off ChitChat was an hourly struggle. It didn't help that in school, I still saw Jameson every day. He was everywhere. Outside the auditorium. In the hallway. Walking across the parking lot. And he never seemed sad.

Not.

At.

All.

I also saw Mariah and her friends, and heard the faint laughter and snarky comments that seemed to trail me wherever I went. I still wondered what people were saying about me online, but I didn't break down and check. I realized that not seeing everything magnified a million times on ChitChat *was* pretty helpful.

Still, though, I missed social media like a constant ache.

It felt so strange not to post selfies with fun filters, or an artfully framed shot of the sky. I wondered what sorts of cool travel posts I was missing.

On Friday afternoon, Luna, Caitlin, and I agreed to meet again in Caitlin's backyard to check in on our progress—no phones allowed. When I got there, Caitlin hadn't arrived yet but Luna sat in an Adirondack chair by the firepit, her book bag at her feet and laptop open on her knees. I knew she had to be working on a school assignment or a newspaper story because laptops were not allowed at these meetings either.

I sat down beside her and pulled my chair close to her to see what she was doing. She was staring at the cursor blinking rhythmically on a blank document.

"What are you working on?" I asked her.

"I'm trying to start an article," she explained.

"About what?"

"Pet ducks."

I frowned. "Because?"

"Mr. Bob, the school resource officer, keeps a duck as a pet," Luna said. "I'm thinking human interest profile? People like animal stories?"

I couldn't keep the lack of enthusiasm off my face. "Maybe you're trying too hard," I said carefully.

Luna shut her laptop in frustration. "I have to submit my article to Tamar in two weeks. I'm running out of time." She turned to me. "I'm never going to be editor in chief, am I?"

"Stop it. You're going to come up with something big enough to write about," I reassured her.

"Everything's been done before. And done better," Luna said, shaking her head.

I put my arm around her. "But not by you."

I could tell that talking about her failure to come up with an idea made her even more stressed. "It's just . . . hard."

"Then why do it?" I asked.

"The school newspaper is more than just a way to make announcements about cheerleading practice," she said, sitting up straight. "It's the voice of the student body and a place for everyone's opinions and ideas. The newspaper allows students to become part of the conversation, not just read about it."

I smiled, and Luna realized she'd been set up. "You did that on purpose."

"I wanted you to remember why you love it so much."

"I do love it," she said, reaching for my hand and squeezing it tight. "Thank you for reminding me." Then she peered at me. "How are *you*?" she asked.

"Not too bad," I said without emotion.

I could tell she wasn't convinced.

At that moment, Caitlin appeared in her backyard. Her cheeks were bright pink, and she walked slowly toward us with her head hanging down. She looked almost as if she'd been crying. My stomach squeezed. Caitlin never cried.

When she reached us, she slumped into the third chair and pulled her feet up, folding into herself. This was bad.

"What's up with you?" Luna asked.

Caitlin hesitated, not answering. Instead, she pulled the laces of her sneakers undone, then retied them. I frowned, looking at her. Something was definitely wrong.

"What happened?" I asked quietly.

Finally, Caitlin said, "I have to tell you guys something."

Luna and I exchanged a worried glance. I braced myself.

"I did something I'm not proud of," Caitlin said, keeping her gaze low. "Just now."

"What is it?" Luna asked.

Caitlin bit her lip like she was trying to keep the words from flying out. When she finally spoke, her voice was shaky and thick. "I went on ChitChat."

What?

I heard Luna gasp, but I sat in shocked silence. Yes, Caitlin was a rule breaker. Yes, keeping this vow was nearly impossible for all of us. But if any of us was going to be the one to crack first, I was certain it would be *me*. Not her.

Caitlin was always the winner in any game. She could keep hidden the longest in hide-and-seek without making a peep. She swung the highest. Ran the fastest. How could she have given up on this so easily? It had practically been her idea in the first place.

"*You?*" I asked at last. "Why?"

Caitlin looked stricken. "The stupid poll," she muttered.

"I thought you were having Davis fill you in on the results," Luna said.

Caitlin shook her head. "It was more than that. See, when I was at football practice this afternoon, during a break, I decided to try to kick a field goal from thirty yards out. And I did it." Happiness and pride flashed across her face, and in spite of everything, I was excited for my friend. "Then I saw that Milo had filmed the whole thing and he told me he was posting it to ChitChat and linking to my poll." She paused and glanced from me to Luna, her eyes pleading for us to understand. "So then I *had* to see what people were saying."

I made a face at the mention of Milo. But I *did* understand how Caitlin must have felt. Why she'd been so curious to look.

"So you reactivated ChitChat?" I said, and Caitlin nodded sheepishly.

"As soon as I got home," she whispered.

I wanted to ask her if she'd checked out Jameson's posts, or Mariah's. If she'd seen people posting more horrible things about me.

"But I *only* looked at the video," Caitlin said, as if reading my mind. "And then the poll. Promise. No other scrolling. And then I deleted the app again."

"What were people saying?" Luna asked flatly. I could tell how disappointed she was in Caitlin, and that made me feel awful, too.

"They loved it," Caitlin whispered with a mix of joy and regret. "Everyone was sharing and liking the video."

"And what about the poll?" I asked. Suddenly, I

remembered that the results were supposed to go up *today*. I held my breath.

Caitlin's face flushed again, but now she looked purely happy. "The results were up. Seventy-five percent voted yes."

"That's amazing!" I cried, momentarily forgetting that she'd broken the vow. I reached over and gave Caitlin a big hug. After a minute, Luna joined in our hug as well.

"It really is amazing," Luna said. "Congratulations, Cait."

"Does this mean you're going to be on the football team?" I asked her as we all pulled free from the hug.

Caitlin shrugged. "I don't know. I'm worried my dad won't let me join. Especially midseason."

"Have you asked him?" I asked.

She shook her head.

"Then it's still game *on*," I said firmly. "You've never been a quitter, so don't start now."

Caitlin flinched. "Well, I quit the vow."

"You did," Luna replied, not letting her off the hook.

"I'm so sorry," Caitlin said, glancing from me to Luna. "Can you guys forgive me?"

"Of course," I said, wanting to be the peacemaker. "People make mistakes." I glanced at Luna. "Right?"

Luna sighed, softening a little. "Right," she said. "I forgive you, too, Cait," she said, and Caitlin's face lit up with a small, grateful smile. "It's not like any of us are perfect," Luna added. "To be totally honest, the thing I'm having the hardest time with isn't even staying off ChitChat. It's the lack of texting."

"That sucks, too," I said, nodding. "Three times a day is *not* enough."

"Maybe we need to come up with a different kind of outlet," Luna said. "A way to express ourselves without texting."

"Like what?" Caitlin asked.

I shrugged. "Sending up flares from our bedroom windows?"

Luna smirked. "Very funny. Maybe we could write stuff down," she said thoughtfully. "But in notebooks. Not on our phones." She put aside her laptop and rummaged inside her backpack before pulling out her trusty notebook. "Sometimes when I'm working on a story and I get stuck, I switch to writing down ideas in my notebook. Something about using a pen and paper helps me think in a different way."

I frowned. "But what kind of stuff would we write?"

"I don't know," Luna said. "Anything. Everything."

Caitlin looked doubtful. "I'm not big on writing down my feelings."

"So, don't," Luna said. "Write whatever you want. I might even share some of my favorite motivational quotes."

Caitlin groaned.

"Not that!" I said.

Luna laughed. "The point is, whenever we feel like posting something or picking up our phones, we write in the notebook instead."

"Who do we write to?" I asked.

"I don't know. The world?" Luna said. "That's who we post to on ChitChat, right?"

The ChitChat comments still swirled around my mind like a whirlpool waiting to suck me down.

"No," I said firmly. "This is a break from social media. Instead of writing to everyone, we write to ourselves."

Caitlin thought about it. "It's like posting to our insides instead of our outsides."

Luna nodded solemnly in agreement. "Exactly."

"Do we show our entries to each other?" Caitlin asked, looking from me to Luna.

"Maybe not at first," Luna said thoughtfully. "We just write for ourselves for now. But maybe later we can share the journals . . . if we feel comfortable." She paused and added, "Not that we have any secrets from each other."

"True," Caitlin said.

"But there's a problem," I finally spoke up, and my friends glanced at me, their eyebrows raised. "We need notebooks. Special ones. For each of us."

Luna grinned. "Shopping trip!"

⟳　⟳　⟳

The Right Card was a shop at the far corner of the square, and the perfect spot for all things journal-y. Before we could get to the journals, though, we were distracted by everything else on offer. The coloring books by the front door immediately attracted Luna's attention, and she oohed and aahed over each one like she'd never colored anything before in her life. Caitlin immediately went to the wall of greeting cards and started reading aloud every corny punch line, ignoring the frowning face of the woman behind the register.

"Look at this one." Caitlin waved me over and I obediently read the jokey birthday card and smiled appropriately. She reluctantly put it back on the shelf. "I love it when Snoopy looks like a vulture on his doghouse," she said.

I left Caitlin to the greeting cards and sniffed my way through a collection of candles. I tried on a soft blue knitted beanie that Luna insisted matched my eyes perfectly, so I decided to buy it for myself as a treat. Caitlin gave up on the cards and went over to convince the woman behind the counter, Mira, to let her taste test the jelly beans. Mira agreed, and I watched as Caitlin carefully selected one bright pink, one purple, and one green jelly bean from the candy counter display. Caitlin put each one in her mouth, one at a time, then slowly chewed while nodding thoughtfully. After the tasting, she discussed the flavors in depth with Mira. Together they decided the green one was not a good choice. Definitely not apple-y enough for either of them. The mixed-berry-smoothie-flavored purple one was a top contender.

"But I have to say Jelly Belly Watermelon is everything summer in one tiny little bite," Caitlin said. "Definitely one of my favorites."

I was surprised to see Mira nod in agreement so enthusiastically she almost shook her tiny yellow reading glasses off her nose. I wanted to laugh. *They bonded over jelly beans?*

Finally, Luna called me toward the back of the store. "Remember what we came for?" she said, holding a leather journal in her hand and flipping through the blank pages.

I nodded and surveyed the shelves. There was every type of journal imaginable—leather, flower-covered, striped, Hello Kitty—and I instantly felt overwhelmed by the choices.

Caitlin joined us in the back of the store, still chewing her jelly beans. "Cool," she said, and reached for a plain red cloth-covered one. "This should work."

"All these options and you pick one just like that?" I asked, impressed and a little envious.

"What?" She looked at me in surprise. "It's what's inside that counts."

I scanned the shelf, looking for inspiration. "I want one that speaks to me," I said. "The outside is important, too."

And then I saw the one. It was a forest-green hardcover, with a gold dragon painted on the front. The letters printed beneath the dragon were gold foil and slick to the touch— *A journal for writing your own story.* I nodded. Fighting dragons was exactly what I needed to do inside this book. My fingers traced the feel of the dragon. It was perfect.

After a lot of debate, Luna finally chose her own journal— a cloth-bound book with pink stripes and big black flowers. She felt the fun look of it would encourage her to write something different from her usual news stories.

"Now let's go pay," Luna said, leading the way back to the counter.

"Wait," I said. "I need a pen."

Caitlin's eyebrows furrowed. "A special pen?"

I nodded. "Exactly."

I wanted strong, bold letters that moved the words across the page and helped me pull the thoughts out of my head. It turned out that Mira had a big pen display behind the counter. It took a few tests on a notepad, but I finally found the pen that glided across the surface and left powerful black marks behind.

"Now I'm ready," I said. I paid for the pen, the journal, and the blue beanie. Caitlin bought a bag of watermelon jelly beans and her journal, and Luna got her journal and a coloring book. The three of us walked out of the store with our new purchases under our arms, and it seemed to me that we all felt a little lighter.

"We did it," Luna said proudly. "Now let the journaling commence!"

Dear Luna,

It seems strange to write to myself without an audience. Just me writing to me. What if I don't have anything to say?

Remember when I was a baby freshman reporter and was assigned to interview five students about what they were looking forward to about the coming school year? It took me every day for two weeks to get five people to stop long enough in the hall to answer my one-question interview. I remember hanging around the bathrooms out by the band hall begging for a couple of sentences from some flute player.

And now here I am, poised to MAYBE be the next editor in chief of the paper. I never thought it could happen this soon for me. But now I'm scared I won't get what I want.

I don't want to write stories about pet ducks or desks. I want to tell the truth. The whole truth. Nothing but the truth. After all, that's what journalism is all about.

But what is my truth?

Luna

⏻ ⏻ ⏻

Hey, you, . . . I mean . . . me,

Why am I always sad watching my father coach his favorite sport? Because I wish it was me running down the field or kicking the ball through the goalposts. I watch the football players with envy, wishing I could be circled up at midfield listening to the quarterback call the plays. It isn't that I don't like soccer—I love soccer—but it seems less important. I seem less important. Not only to my father, but to everyone else at school. The crowds at the football games are easily ten times those at a soccer game. Why can't I be out there in front of the biggest crowd?

I'm taping a tiny piece of grass from the football field on this piece of paper. It was a lot of work and I had the worst time finding Scotch tape in the junk drawer! Did I tell you how much I miss text messages??? Anyway, I pulled these tiny pieces of grass right from the spot where the ball is going to land when I kick the game-winning goal.

☺ Cait

⏻ ⏻ ⏻

People think my sister is named after a city, but she was actually named after grass. My parents met in Africa when they were in the Peace Corps. They named her after the African savanna.

I can't imagine my mom walking out onto the savanna among the wildebeest and giraffe. All she walks with now are the ladies in our neighborhood on their daily coffee runs. And my dad? The biggest adventure he goes on now is going to the gym.

Wildebeest travel long distances across the Serengeti

every year in a great migration. No one tells them when to go or where. They just know they need to travel.

Someday I'm going to travel the world and see animals on safari, and meet many different, wonderful people. And I'm going to see Paris. And maybe I'll fall in love, with someone who loves me as I am. Or maybe I won't. And maybe that's okay.

Annie

CHAPTER EIGHT

Change is painful, but nothing is as painful as staying stuck somewhere you don't belong.

—Mandy Hale

Saturday morning, Savanna knocked on my door way before it was time to go to the bridal shop.

"The store doesn't even open until ten," I grumbled from underneath my covers. She ignored me, bouncing into my room and right into the space of piled pillows beside me.

"Get up. Get up. Get up," she chanted just like I used to do to her every Christmas morning.

I burrowed deeper under the covers and pulled a pillow down over my eyes with a groan. "Five more minutes."

She yanked it off my head and grinned at me. "What do you think of pockets?"

I rubbed my eyes. "Ummm . . . they are . . . good?"

"Exactly." She looked at me like it was a totally normal conversation for a Saturday morning before I'd even had a bowl of cereal. "Pockets are charming *and* useful."

"But," I mumbled, "do we have to talk about them *now*?"

"Of course we do. I have to be ready when they ask me what I'm looking for . . ." Her voice trailed off.

I was confused. "And you're looking for a dress with pockets?"

She laughed. "Among lots of other things, of course. I thought I liked the mermaid silhouette best, but I don't think pockets would work with that shape."

I rolled over on my back, lying beside her. I stared up at the poster on the ceiling. I squinted my eyes, trying to focus on the tip-top of the Eiffel Tower, and wished I was there right now.

"Maybe Miguel and I should go to Paris for our honeymoon," Savanna suddenly said softly, and that definitely got my attention. "What do you think?"

Oh no. I couldn't bear the thought of Savanna seeing Paris before me. Then I felt instantly guilty for being so selfish. Paris should be for everyone.

"Sure," I said weakly.

"Let's take a selfie," Savanna exclaimed, reaching for my phone on the nightstand. "I want to record this day on ChitChat. Hashtag wedding dress shopping with my sis."

Now I was awake. "No," I said sharply, pushing her hand away and sitting up.

Her eyes narrowed. "What's up with you?"

"Nothing." I didn't want to ruin her mood. "I'm taking a break from social media."

Savanna frowned. "Really?"

"It's a temporary thing," I explained, really not wanting to go into detail. "Sort of a school project."

She looked at me, confused. "Is that why you gave me your phone the other night?"

I nodded.

"So I shouldn't tag you in any pics today?"

I shrugged. "I guess you can tag me, but I just can't see the photos you post. At least not now."

"Deal." She sat up in the bed with her legs crossed in front of her. She smoothed the escaped strands of blond hair back into her high ponytail and beamed at me. "I'm just so excited."

"Yeah," I said dryly. "I got that."

Suddenly she smacked her hand against her forehead. "I almost forgot. Did you talk to Jameson about being an usher?" she asked.

My heart dropped. I swallowed hard. "Not yet."

"Well, don't forget. There's just so much to think about; I don't want anyone dropping the ball."

"I was going to ask him, but . . ." I said slowly. I wanted to come clean and tell Savanna about Jameson.

She put her hand up, then took a deep breath. "Never mind. I have to let things go and trust that everyone will do exactly what they are supposed to, right?"

I nodded, silent. Then, as brightly as I could manage, I said, "I'm sorry for not being more excited for you. I know it's a special day and you're going to find the perfect dress."

She grinned back at me and popped out of the bed like

a fluffed-up peacock. "A perfect dress for an absolutely perfect wedding."

Nothing is perfect.

○   ○   ○

The pale blue velvet couch was incredibly uncomfortable with five people jammed onto it. The two high-back brocade chairs facing us sat empty, but no one wanted to be the last one to see Savanna walk out of the dressing room in the next dress option. So far there had been two options—a sparkly ball gown and a mermaid silhouette with a ton of lace—but surprisingly we had all agreed that neither had been *the one*.

Sarah, Savanna's best friend and maid of honor, wiggled her slim hips to squeeze in a little more snugly between me and Savanna's other bridesmaid, Brittney. But I stubbornly held my space at the end of the couch. Sarah and Brittney might be tiny compared to me, but I was the sister of the bride.

"Has she told you anything about the bridesmaid dresses we're wearing?" Sarah asked me.

I shook my head; then Brittney leaned across Sarah. "She told me blue. Very summery. Perfect for June," Brittney said, pushing her thick brown hair back over one shoulder. "Savanna said we could pick out the style we wanted as long as it was the right shade—more cornflower than sapphire, of course."

"Of course," I said, although I had no idea what the difference was.

Brittney seemed to realize how clueless I was because she quickly scrolled through her phone and held out the screen so the whole couch could see the photo of the color swatch. I wished I had my phone on me, but I'd left it at home as a way of combating the constant urge to go back on ChitChat.

"That will be perfect with the flowers," my aunt Edna said from the other end of the crowded couch. She was my mother's older sister and owned a flower shop in town. Weddings were her thing. "I put together some sample arrangements for the bridesmaids' bouquets—iris, hydrangea, yellow roses, and just a touch of white salvia."

She held up her own phone with a photo of the beautiful blue-and-yellow bouquet.

"Oh, Edna, that's lovely," my mom said. "Send that to me."

"To all of us," Brittney chimed in, and Aunt Edna tapped away at her phone.

My hands felt empty. I would have sat on them, but there wasn't enough room on the couch to move.

Sarah was the fashionista of Savanna's group of friends, so I was not surprised she had an opinion on exactly what the dresses should look like. "I think we should all wear something similar in style. Like this." She held out her phone to show us a photo of a halter-style dress with a short ball-gown skirt. Everyone nodded and agreed it was perfect.

Everyone except me.

I swallowed hard.

That dress would look amazing on Sarah and Brittney. But I couldn't imagine standing beside them in front of the whole church wearing something so revealing. Everyone would compare the three of us. I could just imagine the hashtags.

Sarah noticed my reaction. "Of course, you could pick something else if you wanted . . . something more . . . covered," she said as though that would make me feel better. "We don't have to wear the same thing."

There was a commotion from the dressing room, and I was grateful for the interruption. Savanna walked out and stepped up onto the small round stage in front of the full-length mirrors. When she turned around to face us, we all sucked in our breaths.

The strapless dress was simple but elegant. Creamy white lace and organza combined to create a dreamy A-line silhouette. The waist cascaded into a train featuring scalloped lace edges.

We all stared in wonderment at the beautiful girl standing before us. I recognized her. But I didn't. My mom brushed away tears, and Aunt Edna's mouth was wide open. I blinked hard.

This was the girl who whispered ghost stories in my terrified ear when I was only five. And the girl who pushed me off on my wobbly first bicycle ride when I was seven.

And she was definitely the girl who hogged the whole back seat on every car trip.

But now that girl was a bride. I tried to swallow past the lump in my throat as the reality of it all finally hit me.

My sister was getting married.

Newsflash. OLDER SISTER GETS MARRIED AND
YOUNGER SISTER CRIES.

I know. It's not exactly the kind of story I can tell
anyone. I'm a selfish, horrible person for not wanting
Savanna to get married.

But . . .

What happens when I'm the only one in a family of
couples? Do I eat at the countertop because there is no
room for me at the table? Am I destined to sleep on the
pullout sofa in the family room? Will I spend holidays
alone?

Tonight I drew big sad faces on every bride in this
magazine. I can only tell you this, but it made me feel a
little bit better.

Annie

CHAPTER NINE

I am a part of all that I have met.

—Alfred, Lord Tennyson

I sat down in the wingback chair and set my mocha on the table in front of me. I'd come to Mugs coffee shop this afternoon to try writing in my new notebook for a while. Caitlin was at Sunday football practice with her dad, and Luna was at church and then lunch with her family.

I took a sip of mocha, letting the warmth fill my mouth and trickle down my throat. When I finally went to Paris, I would drink *chocolat chaud* and sit at an outdoor café in wooden chairs that wobbled on the cobblestones below my feet. There would be striped awnings over the café windows, and I would see the Eiffel Tower in the distance. I could almost taste the thick, rich hot chocolate I saw in ChitChat pictures, but with a blink, the taste became just a very ordinary mocha again. Everything seemed so far away and impossible to reach.

I glanced around. Most of the brightly painted tables at the coffee shop were full of students studying for exams and future best-selling authors creating their masterpieces. I tensed up for a moment. What if someone here took a picture of me right now and posted it online? I'd look pathetic, just drinking coffee and staring aimlessly into space. They would probably label the photo with hashtags like #loser #nofriends #sadness. I felt the weight of my phone in my purse between my feet, but I didn't reach for it.

Instead, I pulled out my notebook and flipped to a blank page. There were no photos or filters or comments inside. Just empty lines waiting for my own story. I took out my new pen and pulled off the top. I was glad I chose this pen at the store. I loved the thick black line of ink it produced. Serious. Bold. Important.

I'd written a few journal entries so far, but this time I didn't feel like writing to myself. So I wrote to Caitlin, even though I knew she wouldn't see it.

Dear Cait,

How do you become brave? Can you learn it like you learn the rules to soccer or football? Are there drills and exercises? I know I'm just a huge pity party, but I keep wondering what I could have done to make things turn out differently. Could I be different? Can anyone?

Annie

My pen stopped, and I looked up from the page to glance out the window. Old Town was crowded today. The wind had more fall than summer in it, and everyone seemed to have come out to enjoy the chill in the air. Coats were on and scarfs were wrapped tighter, and a steady stream of people paraded by on the leaf-strewn sidewalks, caught up in their own little lives. Couples holding hands. Families with strollers and toddlers. College kids laughing in groups.

Everyone looked so happy.

I wanted to be happy again.

No one ever told me a broken heart would feel like a panic attack, always striking when least expected. Anything could bring it on: Whiffs of certain smells. Specific shades of colors. Lingering tastes of once-shared dishes. But mostly places.

Out on the square, a kid flew by on a skateboard, and without warning, the memory came, vicious and excruciating.

I remembered the first time Jameson kissed me. It was last fall and still so hot the sweat was trickling down the backs of my bare legs. We were eating takeout pizza on a bench outside CooperSmith's and listening to a bluegrass band playing on the outdoor stage. The sun was just starting to disappear behind the tops of the redbrick buildings, and there was the slightest of breezes starting up. Strings of white lights lit up the kids screaming and dodging the splashes of water that spurted unpredictably up into the air. I was laughing at something. Jameson was watching me, and then he leaned in and kissed me. Quick. Light. Perfect.

He loved me. I knew he did.

He just didn't anymore.

And then I saw him.

There he was now, outside the window. Jameson. I couldn't believe it. He was on the other side of the street, standing with his hands deep in his jeans pockets. He was wearing the T-shirt I gave him for Christmas and the Nike sneakers he saved up months to buy.

My mouth quivered. I tucked back into the chair, hoping he didn't see me. My brain buzzed, and I felt as if all the air was suddenly sucked out of the room. What would the people walking by think if the girl sitting in the coffee shop window suddenly stood up and began pounding at the glass?

Hey, it's me. Remember? Me?

Jameson liked me so much, and now he didn't anymore. Did that mean I wasn't likable? Was I less attractive? Were all those awful comments right? Was this all my fault?

I had so many questions.

Suddenly, Jameson smiled and lifted his hand in greeting. I followed his gaze and saw Milo walking toward him. I felt a flare of anger. Of course. I guessed he and Milo were besties now, after that whole video takedown they'd planned together. I wanted to pull out my phone and search Jameson's ChitChat account. I needed to know what he was doing—or at least I thought I did. Now I watched them greet each other with a fist bump, then walk off toward the square, laughing and talking.

The two of them disappeared from view. But I didn't want to stay at Mugs anymore. I stuffed my notebook into my purse, then stood up and left the half-empty mocha on the table by the window.

○   ○   ○

On the way home, I drove past the high school. The lights on the field were still on even though Sunday practice was long over. I parked the car and let myself in through the gate by the locker rooms. The field was eerily quiet. The floodlight illuminated a wide swath of grass in front of the goalposts, like a stage ready for the performance to begin. I'd never seen it so empty before, but I could almost hear the roar of the crowd and the impact as the players slammed each other to the ground. I hadn't been to a game yet this season, but I'd accompanied Caitlin to so many games over the years.

I was wrong. The field was not completely empty. Caitlin stood beside the tee on the twenty-yard line, three footballs laid out on the grass.

"Annie?" she called when she saw me.

"I thought I might find you here," I said. "Do you want some company? Because I do."

Caitlin nodded. "Practicing helps keep me off ChitChat."

"Good plan," I said. "I need a distraction, too." I walked past her to take up a position behind the goalposts. "I can fetch the balls."

Caitlin laughed. Then she grew serious and set the first football on the tee. She squinted, concentrating, and swung her leg back. The first kick sent the ball off to the right, and the second kick was too short, making the ball bounce onto the grass and roll slowly to a stop. Caitlin looked frustrated.

"That's okay!" I yelled, trying to think of what I'd heard her dad say at practices. "You need to work the jitters out."

Caitlin put the last ball on the tee and squinted at it. Her foot connected solidly, and this time the ball went sailing in a perfect spiral through the center of the goalposts.

"Caitlin!" I cried, clapping. "You did it!"

I ran to retrieve the balls, then ran back toward her and gave her a big hug. "You're amazing," I said. "You should totally be on the team." I paused, then added, "Have you asked your dad yet?"

Caitlin shook her head. After a moment, we sat down together on the grass. I sensed Caitlin needed to talk.

"All my childhood was spent learning not to do things 'like a girl,'" she said finally. She picked a piece of grass and studied it. "So now I don't throw like a girl or run like a girl. But it doesn't change things. I can't play football because I'm a girl."

"You need to talk to your dad," I said firmly.

Caitlin shrugged. "After Mom died, Dad and I tried to learn to talk again. Sometimes he answers with one word, but sometimes he actually carries on a conversation. Even laughs."

"Your mom was great at talking," I said, remembering Caitlin's mom with a sad smile. "About everything and nothing at all."

"Football is the only thing my dad and I really talk about." Caitlin wiped the tears from the corners of her eyes, then smiled at me. "I don't want to cry like a girl."

"Everybody cries." I didn't tell her I'd cried all the way from the coffee shop to the football field.

She tilted her head slightly, thinking hard. "So, you'll help me talk to my dad?"

"How am I supposed to do that?"

"Just be there when I do it. He's always liked you . . ." Her hazel eyes were big and hopeful. "Pleeeeeeease."

"Okay, okay," I said. "I'll be there for you when you ask him."

"Thanks, Annie," Caitlin said. "Where would I be without you?"

I sighed. "Well, you'd probably still be on ChitChat, for one," I replied.

Caitlin started laughing. "Maybe it's not such a bad thing to be off it. Even if I *am* still wondering what people are saying about the video Milo posted."

"Who cares about the video?" I said. "What I just saw right now? That's better than any video." Caitlin smiled, bumping my shoulder. "And I bet I can guess what people would be saying on ChitChat, too."

"Yeah?" Caitlin asked.

I nodded, tilted my head back, and cupped my hands

over my mouth. I yelled words into the dark like comments scrolling across the sky.

"IF THIS IS THE GIRL THAT WANTS ON THE
TEAM, THEN ABSOLUTELY!!!!! WOW!

"SIGN THAT GIRL UP!!

"HEY, COACH! SEND HER IN!!!!"

I knew I looked and sounded silly, but it was worth it
to hear Caitlin laugh, and to laugh with her.

Maybe we'd be okay without ChitChat after all.

CHAPTER TEN

The world is round and the place which may seem like the end may also be only the beginning.

—Ivy Baker Priest

Every morning, I still woke up and reached for my phone before I remembered I couldn't log on to ChitChat. Monday morning was no different. I woke up, picked up the phone, but then carefully placed it on my nightstand. I still wasn't used to the empty feeling.

When I came downstairs and walked into the kitchen, my father was there looking lost. He had the cabinet under the sink open and was staring blankly at the trash can. He was still in his pajamas.

"Where is the dish soap?" he mumbled.

"It's on the counter," I answered him. He finally looked around as though he was seeing me for the first time.

"Oh." He straightened, picked up the dish soap, and squirted some into the sink. I didn't tell him he should really run the water first and then put the soap in the sink.

"Do you have work today?" I asked.

"I have a dentist appointment," he said. "I'm going in later."

I nodded and poured Frosted Flakes into a clean bowl, then added milk and grabbed a spoon. I sat down at the table and shoveled cereal into my mouth. Dad sat down at the table across from me with a cup of coffee and a granola bar. The difference without a phone in my hand was startling. It was almost like I needed to say something out loud. *But what?* I took another bite of cereal. *What did we used to talk about before I had a phone?*

"This wedding is a really big deal to your sister," my dad finally said, startling me.

"I know."

He looked at me for a long time, frowning slightly. "Do you think . . . " He paused, as if he was thinking really hard about something. As if he was choosing his words very carefully. ". . . I really have to wear a tuxedo?"

I smiled. My dad was definitely not the tuxedo type. He was much more the tattoos, jeans, and T-shirt type. But I was surprised he was worried about it.

"You're going to look great in a tux, Dad," I said.

"You think?"

When do you stop worrying about how you look? Does it ever go away?

My dad took a sip of coffee. The hummingbird tattoo on his wrist hovered above his cup like the birds used to do at the back porch feeder.

"Savanna said I'm supposed to give a speech at the reception," he said.

"Dad, the wedding isn't until June," I said. "You have plenty of time to figure out what to say."

"I know," he said, and groaned. "I'm just thinking about it."

"More like worrying about it."

He shrugged sheepishly. "I wish I could keep you both little for a while longer. I don't think I'm ready for you to grow up."

I thought about my dad being surrounded by girls all his life. It must have been hard sometimes. Then I thought about Caitlin and her dad. "Did you ever wish I was a boy?" I asked.

"I have never wanted you to be a boy. Never." He looked at me straight on. Were those tears in his eyes? My dad, crying? Slowly he reached out across the table and stroked my cheek.

"I just wish I understood girls a little bit better and all that . . . stuff . . . you go through." He smiled sheepishly.

"I wish I did, too, Dad."

I stood up from my chair and walked around the table. He looked up at me with a half smile, and I put my arms around him, hugging him tight.

"You will be an amazing father of the bride," I said.

◑　◑　◑

In English class that day, we had a pop quiz on *The Great Gatsby*. Our teacher, Mr. Stein, walked down the aisles, handing out the tests and giving us a thumbs-up for encouragement.

Mr. Stein looked like he could have still been in high school himself. He was short and stocky, his round eyes always blinking rapidly behind steel-rimmed glasses.

The one good thing about being off ChitChat was that I'd had more time to read. I'd finished *The Great Gatsby* in practically one sitting and loved it.

I looked down at the paper on my desk, reading the prompt for the essay we were supposed to write.

In the novel, Gatsby has difficulty accepting that the past is over and done with. How does he try to recapture the past? What does this say about him? Should people live their lives longing for something in the past? Why or why not?

I stared down at the words. I thought of my dad, how he wanted to keep Savanna and me in the past. Maybe I was doing the same thing with Jameson.

If only it were easier to move on.

⏻   ⏻   ⏻

That afternoon, at Caitlin's request, I waited with her after school until her dad was done with practice. When Caitlin and I got into her dad's car, I could see how nervous she was. She was going to ask her dad about joining the football team on the ride home. I held my breath and gave her a supportive nod. I just hoped this wouldn't be too awkward.

Caitlin's dad drove off, navigating the parking lot and ignoring the buzz of his phone on the seat. This time of the year his phone was always full of messages from players, parents, and even teachers. Everyone focused on the possibility of a winning season courtesy of Coach Stone. Our team had been racking up wins, even though we'd lost the most recent game.

Before Caitlin could say anything, her dad spoke up.

"I thought we'd go out for dinner tonight. Want to join us, Annie?" he asked.

"Ummm . . . I have a lot of homework."

Caitlin shot me a look.

"But sure. I'd love to."

Caitlin smiled. "How about Austin's?" she asked. It was a restaurant in Old Town we both liked. Her dad nodded, humming to himself.

As we approached Austin's, Caitlin sat up straight and spoke.

"So, I was watching Eli kicking today."

"And?" her dad said, his eyes on the road.

"I have an idea," Caitlin said. She took a deep breath and continued, "Eli might need a backup."

"We don't have one."

Her dad turned into the parking lot at Austin's, turned off the engine, and twisted to face her. The sudden tension between them made my stomach tighten.

"I could do it," Caitlin said. Her voice came out quiet. Unlike her.

Her dad's expression hardened. "We don't have girls on the team."

"I'm better than him. You know it."

"Maybe. But you're a girl."

"Duh."

He frowned at her sarcasm.

"And that's the only reason I can't be on the team? Because I'm a girl?"

"It's one reason, but not the main one. I don't want you to get hurt." His tone left little room for argument. But I glanced at Caitlin's face. I knew what she was thinking. She had gone this far and wasn't going to give up easily. Her dad had taught her that.

"I can get hurt playing soccer," she argued.

"It's not the same thing. People aren't hitting you. Knocking you down. Running over you."

Her voice got louder. "Accidents happen, Dad. You can't keep me from getting hurt."

I realized I was holding my breath again. Maybe they'd just forgotten I was back here?

"There's a video posted online," Caitlin's dad finally said. "Of you. I think Milo posted it, but someone forwarded it to me."

Caitlin nodded.

"You're kicking field goals. Over and over again. Right through the goalposts."

Caitlin's eyes widened, and my heart started to beat faster. *And?*

Her dad sighed. "You're good, Cait. I'm not going to deny that. And it's not that I don't think you can do it. I know you can." He rubbed his eyes. "It's just, you're five foot five and one hundred twenty pounds. What if a guy twice your size gets through the return coverage on the kickoff? What if three big guys come at you to block a point after?"

"Dad, you know all the bad things that *might* happen . . . more than anyone else," Cait pleaded, "but there are over two thousand girls playing high school football in this country." It seemed Cait had done some Luna-style research of her own. "I want to be one of them."

"The dad in me says absolutely not," her dad said, then paused. "But as a coach, I know we need a backup."

My heart took off at the realization of what her dad had just said.

"And?" Caitlin asked.

"I could bring up Jack Richardson from the junior varsity team."

Oh.

Caitlin's eyebrows shot up. "Jack hasn't made a single goal. Not in a real game."

Her dad looked pained because he knew she was right. "He hit a couple in practice."

There was a long silence between them. I knew Caitlin was dying to say more, but somehow she held it in. Saying the wrong thing wasn't an option.

Her dad opened the car door, and the three of us got out of the car and walked in awkward silence over to Austin's. The waiter sat us in a booth and brought us water and menus. I was sitting beside Caitlin, and we both looked

across at her dad. I couldn't quite tell what he was thinking. Finally, he spoke again.

"You could get hurt out there," he said.

"I could get hurt on the sidewalk." Caitlin motioned out
the window. "I could be hurt on the soccer field. Life is
full of risks."

Caitlin's dad was quiet for a minute, fiddling with his
menu. Beneath the table, I clasped Caitlin's hand, hoping
he'd say yes.

Eventually, her dad stared at Caitlin across the table,
and nodded.

"Okay," he said.

Okay?

"Okay?" Caitlin whispered, her eyes shining.

"I'll give you a tryout," her dad said. "Just like everyone else. No special treatment," he added.

"Of course not," Caitlin said, and a huge grin spread
across her face. I could feel myself start to grin, too. This
was actually happening.

"On one condition."

"Yes?" Caitlin asked.

He gave her a look. "On that field, I'm the coach."

Cait nodded frantically. "Got it."

"If I don't send you into the game, there's a reason for
it. You have to trust my judgment."

Caitlin nodded again, not daring to say anything that
might mess things up.

Her dad took a deep breath, then mumbled, "I don't even know if we have a uniform that will fit you."

Caitlin slid out of the booth and went over to her dad, giving him a quick hug and a kiss on the top of the head.

"You won't be sorry. I won't let you down," she insisted.

"You never do," he said.

⏻ ⏻ ⏻

After dinner, all I wanted to do was share Caitlin's good news on ChitChat. I thought about what I would have posted—a selfie of me and Cait and her dad, with the hashtags #footballteam #makinghistory. I imagined all the likes and comments that would pour in, and how people like Milo and Jameson and Mariah would react. I thought about it the whole time that Caitlin's dad drove us back home from Austin's. But I didn't touch my phone.

I waved good night to Cait and her dad and got out of their car. I let myself inside my house and went upstairs to my room.

When my parents first moved into the neighborhood, my dad planted tiny blue spruce trees along the fence line. Now the trees were tall enough to block the view into our living room. But my bedroom on the second floor was still perfectly unobstructed and aligned with Luna's room.

Tonight I saw her clearly, standing in her window in her fleece pajamas. She saw me, too, and smiled. She held both hands over her head with her fingers spread wide.

It was our long-ago-designed way of asking to come over before any of us had access to phones and text messages. I gave a thumbs-up: the response that meant yes, of course. A thumbs-down was no, but I almost never gave that.

It was a relief to know Luna would be coming over. I had felt *this* close to breaking the vow. Now I'd have a distraction.

I was sitting up in bed, flipping through one of Savanna's bridal magazines, when Luna arrived a few minutes later wearing an oversized T-shirt and leggings. She kicked off her fleece-lined boots and threw herself across the empty side of the bed.

"Cait got her dad to let her try out for the team," I told Luna, and she cheered.

"That's the kind of thing Cait *would* have posted on ChitChat," Luna said, plumping up one of my pillows behind her head.

I flipped a page of *Modern Bride* and nodded. "I would have posted about it, too."

"How's the wedding planning going?" Luna asked, looking at the picture on the cover of the veiled woman tossing a bouquet of lilies over one shoulder.

"It's going well," I said, closing the magazine. "Savanna's really excited."

Luna squinted her eyes at me. "So why don't you look happy about it?"

"I was thinking about how it's never going to be just

me and Savanna anymore. Now everybody is paired up. Even my mom and dad have each other. I'm going to be the odd one out in my own family. It feels . . . weird."

"Maybe you can write about it in your journal," Luna suggested.

"How is that working for you?" I asked.

"Not great. I still want to go on ChitChat every few minutes. I think about it all the time."

"I was *dying* to break the vow tonight," I confessed. "I almost did."

"Why was tonight so tough?"

I shrugged. "I guess I was excited for Cait . . . and also I just keep wondering what I'm missing on there. Even though I know going online will probably make me feel bad about myself, I still want to do it." I pulled my purple floral comforter up under my chin. "It doesn't make sense."

"FOMO," Luna said. "Fear of missing out. It's a social anxiety people have about being disconnected from others."

"It's a real thing?" I felt better knowing I wasn't alone.

She nodded. "Being off social media can make FOMO worse for people who feel like they are missing opportunities."

"Seriously, how do you know all this stuff?" I asked.

She laughed. "Wikipedia. It's my weakness."

"I miss Jameson," I said quietly. "I needed to tell someone."

"I'm glad it was me," she said, putting her head on my shoulder. "And not ChitChat."

"Me too," I said, leaning my head against hers. "Hey, did I ever tell you how great you are for going offline for me?"

"No."

We sat quietly for a moment.

"So . . . ?"

"So . . . what?" I asked.

"Tell me!"

I rolled my eyes, then said, "Luna Ortega is pretty great."

"Thanks," Luna said with a grin. "I 'like' that comment."

I have to admit something about myself. I figured it out last night when I was just lying in bed waiting (and waiting . . . and waiting) to fall asleep. Usually, I would be scrolling through ChitChat looking at pictures, reading comments and posts. But now I just think.

So here's the thing. I do things sometimes because of the audience. Every like, or comment, or mention makes me feel like I matter. Is that so bad?

Social media asks so many questions. It implores me to answer.

How are you feeling?

What are you doing?

Where are you?

Who are you with?

What makes you angry?

But I need somewhere to answer them.

Annie

⏻　⏻　⏻

When I was a kid, I remember lying on my back on the living room floor with my feet a couple of inches above the carpet. I held my feet up, until my legs shook from the effort, while my dad sat beside me with a stopwatch to measure my progress. Eventually my legs grew stronger and I could hold them up longer and longer. My father was so happy with me.

"That's better," he'd say with satisfaction as he clicked the button on the stopwatch. "But it's not good enough."

And then one day, as I was almost about to break my

all-time record and was feeling unusually satisfied, my father took a dictionary off the bookshelf on the living room wall and balanced it carefully on top of my suspended ankles.

My feet immediately fell to the floor with a thump.

I was good. But I wasn't good enough.

Cait

○ ○ ○

You know what's silly? I miss posting GIFs. And funny videos. Like the ones where a cat is trying to jump on something and they fail miserably. But they keep trying. Isn't that what life is supposed to be about? What else is there?

One time I saw a video of a donkey that was losing his freaking mind when he saw his owner come to the fence. It made me cry. Not like sob or anything, but I teared up. Over a donkey I didn't even know!!

This vow is so hard to keep.

Luna

CHAPTER ELEVEN

The heart will break, but broken live on.

—Lord Byron

The next day after school, Caitlin texted me and Luna to meet her in Mugs. We knew she'd had her football team tryout today, and obviously she wanted to tell us the news in person, whether it was good or bad.

While we waited for Caitlin, Luna and I sat at one of the tables by the window. Luna was working on another article on her laptop, but she wasn't making much progress. I sat doodling in my notebook and sipping a latte.

Finally, Caitlin burst into the café, her hair still damp from the shower and her face glowing with big news.

"I made it," Caitlin announced, running over to me and Luna. "The football team!"

"Congrats!" I exclaimed, and jumped up to join in the hug Luna was already giving Caitlin.

"This is *amazing*," Luna said. "You are the first girl ever to play varsity football at Fort Collins High School."

"I knew you could do it," I said quietly. I leaned over and put my head on Caitlin's shoulder. "When do you start?"

"I start practice with the team right away, but I get to suit up and be on the field for the next game. The one right after the pep rally!"

"You're going to be a star," I proclaimed.

The three of us sat back down at the table, making room for Caitlin.

"I don't know about being a *star*." Caitlin frowned. "I'll probably spend most the season sitting on the bench. I'm still only the backup kicker."

"You won't be a backup for long," I assured her, sipping my latte.

"Do you want to know something?" Caitlin said after a moment. Luna and I nodded. "As happy as I am, all I want to do is post the news all over ChitChat." She shrugged, looking disappointed in herself. "But I haven't broken the vow again. And I won't. I promise."

"I know you won't," Luna said. "But I get it. I'm missing ChitChat a lot, too."

"I almost broke the vow last night," I told Caitlin. "I wanted to share your news, too!"

"I had an idea after I got back from Annie's place last night," Luna said. She glanced from Caitlin to me. "Remember how the meditating helped us? And writing in the notebook helps me, too."

"Yeah, the notebook is kind of growing on me," I admitted, and Caitlin nodded.

"Well, I think we need to try more things like that," Luna declared. "Things we can choose to do *instead* of going on ChitChat."

"Like . . . sports?" Caitlin offered.

I shook my head. "It should be something different from

things we normally might do," I said, feeling suddenly inspired. "Like, I don't know, volunteering someplace?"

"That's cool," Luna said. She opened a new document on her laptop and started typing. "What else?"

Caitlin pulled her feet up onto her chair and wrapped her arms around her knees. "Maybe we could even just . . . play. In our backyards. Like when we were kids." She blushed. "Is that stupid?"

Luna tapped at the keyboard. "I'll put it down anyway. Remember, no ideas are bad. We're just brainstorming."

"Okay," I said, thinking for a minute. "Maybe we could take a lesson of some sort? Like an art class?"

"That's a good one." Luna typed furiously.

And that was how the list took shape. Simple things. Hard things. Silly things. Until the page was full of ways to spend time doing something—anything—except going online.

When it was done, Luna turned her computer around and showed it to us:

Things to Do Offline
- Volunteer
- Play
- Take a lesson
- Write a poem
- Read a book
- Go on a hike
- Organize your closet
- Call someone you love

- Watch a favorite movie
- Be a tourist in your own town
- Dye your hair
- Go on a picnic
- Fix something that's broken

"I think we should pick one that we all do together," Luna said. "And then we can each do our own things, of course."

"Okay, but which one should be our first joint activity?" Caitlin asked.

"We'll never agree on one," I said. "There's only one fair way to do this."

I closed my eyes and pointed to a spot on the screen at random. I heard Luna squeal and Caitlin gasp. I opened my eyes.

Dye your hair.

Uh-oh. I loved my blond hair. "Let me pick again," I said.

"No, this is perfect," Luna said. "I think we need to go bold with something that symbolizes our vow. Something that reminds us every day that we are in this together."

"I don't know," I said dubiously.

"On Saturday morning, we dye our hair bright pink," Luna declared.

"Pink hair? No way," Caitlin said emphatically.

"You don't have to dye all of it," Luna said. "Just a streak. And it's not permanent. "

"I'll think about it," Caitlin said.

"I'm in," I said. Maybe a new look would help me get a new perspective. "My sister's favorite salon is in Old Town. I'll make us all an appointment. If we're going to do this, we might as well get the help of a professional."

And since I was feeling brave, I decided I'd tackle another option on my own. It was the first thing I'd suggested for the list—volunteering someplace. And I had just the place in mind.

CHAPTER TWELVE

Isn't it nice to think that tomorrow is a new day with no mistakes in it yet?

—L. M. Montgomery

The boy behind the desk at the animal shelter when I walked in on Wednesday looked vaguely familiar. He had a gray stocking cap pulled low over his dark eyes. I realized he went to Fort Collins High School. A senior? Just my luck. After selecting a volunteer opportunity that was supposed to be full of animals—*not* people—I immediately run into someone I know. Sort of. The tag on the ribbon around his neck said his name was Isco.

"That's unusual," I mumbled, suddenly worried he would recognize me from the ChitChat video. I couldn't escape no matter what I did.

He looked up from watering the ivy behind the counter. "The plant?" he asked.

"No." I blushed. "Your name."

"It's short for Francisco. Like the Spanish soccer player?"

I stared hopelessly at him.

"Not a soccer fan?"

I shook my head. "Not really."

"That's okay. I don't play soccer. And I'm Filipino, not Spanish," he said.

I momentarily forgot my purpose. "Do you speak . . . Filipino?"

"My parents speak Tagalog, and no, I don't speak it well," he answered. "What about you?"

"Me?" I was confused.

"Your name?"

Whew. Maybe he didn't recognize me?

"Oh," I said. "I'm Annie. I'm named after my grandmother—Annie Macleod. She was from Scotland."

"Do you speak Scottish?"

"Touché," I said. "Point made. It was a stupid question."

He put down the watering can and perched on a barstool behind the counter.

"How can I help you, Annie?" he asked.

"I'd like to volunteer," I told him.

He leaned over the counter, resting his elbows on the knees of his faded jeans.

"Wonderful. There's an orientation Saturday."

I bit my lip. Saturday was the salon appointment with my friends. I couldn't bail on them.

"I don't think I can make it Saturday," I said sadly. Maybe volunteering wasn't in the cards for me.

"Well." Isco looked at me. "We don't turn volunteers away. If you're determined to do it today, you could read to the dogs."

"Read?" I asked. "Aloud?"

"It gets them more comfortable with people. All you have to do is sit outside the kennel and read. You can do that, right?"

"I'm not sure I even like dogs," I blurted. Probably not the best idea to admit that out loud. But the truth was, I didn't know what I did and didn't like anymore.

"If you don't like it, you can come back up here and we'll try something different. Don't worry," Isco said, with a warm smile. "There's plenty of jobs to do around here. Some with dogs, some without."

"Thanks," I said. "What should I read?"

"Anything you want. Your homework. Your favorite novel. A picture book. It doesn't matter. It's about the dogs getting used to people's voices. Do you have something in there?" He gestured toward my backpack.

My phone was in there, but I also had plenty of schoolbooks. I nodded.

"Okay," Isco said. "I'll show you the way."

I took a deep breath, then followed him through a heavy door and down a wide tiled walkway. Most of the kennels were occupied. There were jumpy, barking dogs eager to meet anyone walking down the corridor. Little dogs. Medium dogs. Fluffy dogs. Finally, we stopped at a kennel at the end of the hall. The dog inside was a big Labrador mix, curled into a ball on a bed in the corner. When I stopped in front of the fence, his eyes immediately looked up at my face, questioning. But he didn't get up and come to the gate.

"This is Rocco," Isco said. The dog lifted his head slightly at the sound of his name, but he still didn't move from the bed.

"Is he all right?" I asked.

"He will be. With your help."

"He looks sad," I said.

"He's going to be fine," Isco told me. "He's just grieving. Dogs feel loss, too."

"Do I have to go inside the pen?" I asked nervously.

"Not if you don't want to. But he's not aggressive," Isco said. "He likes you. I can tell."

There was nothing in Rocco's deep brown eyes to indicate he even noticed me, much less liked me. "Why would he like me? He's never even seen me before."

Isco shrugged. "Maybe it's something about how you smell. Maybe you remind him of someone. Who knows?"

I looked at the dog. He looked back at me. "What's wrong with him?" I asked.

"He's fine, physically. I think he's just sad."

I know how he feels, I thought.

"Here's a blanket for you to sit on." Isco spread it out in the hallway in front of the fence gate. "I can stay with you awhile if you want."

"No," I said. "I'll be fine."

"If you need anything, just come back up to the front desk." He turned and started up the hallway, calling over his shoulder. "I'll be there."

I settled down on the blanket, laying my backpack beside me. Still Rocco didn't move. I fidgeted, trying to think about what I should read. Finally, I unzipped the backpack and dug around inside. Chemistry didn't seem interesting enough to read even to a dog, nor did geometry or even history. But then my fingers touched a small paperback at the bottom of the bag. I forgot it was there—a guidebook to Paris. Savanna had given it to me as a gift for my last birthday, and I'd started carrying it around in my bag.

I pulled the book out, and it fell open to a section about the Arc de Triomphe. It seemed like as good a spot to start reading as anywhere.

I took a deep breath, then started reading aloud softly. "'The Arc de Triomphe de l'Étoile is one of the most famous monuments in Paris, France, standing at the western end of the Champs-Élysées at the center of Place Charles de Gaulle . . .'"

I finished that section quickly, then moved on to read a section about Luxembourg Gardens because surely any dog would love to hear about the lawns, tree-lined promenades, and flower beds at one of the most beautiful gardens in the world. When I finally looked up from the book, I was surprised to see Rocco lying by the gate just inches from my knee. He was a big dog, probably eighty pounds, but I hadn't heard him move.

His eyes were like milk chocolate, and he looked at me like he was memorizing my face. Slowly, carefully, I put my fingers through the fence. His eyes followed my movements, but he stayed completely still. I patted him gently on the head, and slowly Rocco closed his eyes.

"I know some people say it's overrated, but we should

read the part about the Eiffel Tower, don't you think?" I asked Rocco, and was rewarded with a tiny twitch of his long brown tail. "I'll take that as a yes."

I settled in a little more comfortably and turned another page, holding up the picture for Rocco to consider. "'The Eiffel Tower was named after the architect Gustave Eiffel and completed in 1889. The tower was supposed to be a temporary arched entrance for the World's Fair, but the French fell in love and insisted it remain standing. Now it is one of the most famous monuments in all the world. Every night on the hour, twenty thousand lights twinkle for five minutes.'"

I closed my eyes for a minute, remembering the ChitChat video I saw once of the lights on the tower. Magical. A soft nuzzle against the fence brought me back to reality. Rocco looked worried, his furry doggy eyebrows lowered in concern.

"Don't worry," I told him. "I'm still here. I was just thinking of places far away from here. It's kind of my thing."

His ears rose a little, and he tilted his head like he was thinking about what I said. I suddenly realized while he might not dream of the Eiffel Tower, he might know what it felt like to want to be away from here. He might be thinking of faraway places he only dreamed about—like fields of grass and cozy couches.

I closed up the book and stuffed it back into my backpack. Rocco seemed to know I was leaving and moved silently to the bed in the corner of the kennel. It was like he couldn't bear to see me actually walk away.

"I'll be back," I whispered through the fence. But when I left, a part of my heart stayed behind in the kennel at the end of the hall.

Outside in the parking lot, the wind had a cold nip of a Colorado fall, and I dragged the folds of my forest-green coat around my body. The gust of wind blew me in the direction of my car. Stopping in front of the blue Honda, I struggled to untangle my windblown hair from my face so I could dig in my purse for the car keys.

I slid inside and turned the key. Click. Something was not right. I tried again. Click. *No. No. No.* I put my head down on the steering wheel.

The tap at the window made me jump.

"You need some help?" Isco stood outside.

I rolled the window down. "I could call someone." Even as I said it, I knew it sounded lame.

"Or you could just let me help."

"I know how to use jumper cables."

"I figured you did," he said. "But the thing about jumper cables is that you need a car on the other end."

"I know that."

I knew I was being snippy with my answers. It wasn't his fault exactly, but I didn't want Isco to be nice right now and I certainly didn't want him to be the one on the other end of the jumper cables.

After a minute, Isco pulled a black Jeep around to the front of my car, then slid out and opened his hood. I got out of my car and walked over to him with my jumper cables. He took them and fastened them onto his battery.

"How did it go with Rocco?" he asked, his eyes still on the connections.

"Fine." I opened the hood of my car and attached the other end of the cables.

He walked back to his car and slid into the driver's seat, gunning the motor. "You can try it now," he called out the open door.

I know that. I got in my car, turned the key, and the motor roared to life. I was almost disappointed. I hadn't wanted Isco to have the spark that saved the day, but what were my options? To sit here in the cold out of pure stubbornness?

Isco was already out of the Jeep and pulling the cables off the batteries.

"Thanks," I said.

He wrapped the cables up and handed them to me. "Sometimes it helps when I'm stuck to talk about it," he said. "So I'm up for hanging out sometime and talking about it."

I didn't feel like hanging out or talking with anyone.

"I'm good," I said, slamming the hood of my car down for emphasis and walking back to the driver's seat.

CHAPTER THIRTEEN

Do you know what my favorite part of the game is? The
opportunity to play.

—Mike Singletary

I sat on the grass watching as Caitlin shook her hands out
in the chilly night air to warm them up. This was just her
first official practice with the team, but I could tell she
still felt the nerves. She bounced up and down on her toes,
then sat down on the grass beside me to stretch out her
legs. I wasn't used to seeing her in the football uniform,
with the padded shoulders and all. But she looked good.
Really good.

"I'm proud of you," I said, thinking it was the least I
could do to keep her company on the sidelines. Luna had
wanted to come, too, but she was off chasing a new possible story for the paper.

"I haven't done anything yet," Caitlin pointed out.

"But you're here, right?" I said.

"Looking hot in that jersey, Cait." Davis walked over
and gave Caitlin an exaggerated wink.

She rolled her eyes at him. "Ditto, jerk."

Davis laughed. He sat down beside us, setting his helmet on the grass. "You ready for this?" he asked Caitlin.

"As ready as I'll ever be," Caitlin said, bending from the waist to stretch toward her toes.

"Have you seen all the commotion you're causing?" Davis asked.

I glanced over at him. "What are you talking about?"

"There's like a million posts about Cait being on the team," he told me, then glanced back at Caitlin. "You're a ChitChat star."

She shook her head vigorously. "I can't look."

"Honestly, it's not all bad," he told her.

Caitlin tucked a stray piece of hair behind her ear. "I'm sure there are plenty of haters on there. Don't need that in my head."

"Besides," I said, "we took a vow to stay offline."

Davis raised his eyebrows at me. "Why?"

"It started out as a way to support me," I explained.

"That video of Jameson?" Davis asked.

I nodded. There was no hiding what had happened.

Caitlin reached for her left ankle and pulled her body down toward her leg, her face almost brushing against her knee. "That was how it started," she said. "But now I feel like staying offline will help me concentrate on being a better player. I need total focus."

I felt strengthened by what she said. Maybe the vow *was* a good thing and not just about me.

But the truth was, I'd felt more tempted than ever lately to go back on ChitChat.

"It's not easy being the coach's daughter," Caitlin went

on. "Everyone thinks I made the team because my dad's giving me a break. You don't know what it's like to have people watching and criticizing everything you do."

"Seriously?" Davis looked at her and shook his head incredulously. "You do know I'm a gay, black football player, right?"

"Of course I do," Caitlin said. She blinked, then went quiet. This was massive. Davis never opened up like this, and neither of us wanted to shut him down.

Davis kept talking, his jaw tight. "Facing a rushing row of linebackers wanting to smash me to the ground is easy compared to the people who come for me every single day online."

I nodded. "But do you care what random people think?" I asked him.

"Doesn't everybody?" He considered me for a moment. "Everybody has their own stuff. Nobody is immune to the meanness."

I knew he was right. I folded my legs up and looked toward the bleachers. Some kids were hanging out there to watch the practice game. I spotted Mariah and Jordyn sitting side by side. Mariah wore a red skirt and an oversized denim jacket. Jordyn had on a red puffer jacket the exact shade of Mariah's skirt. The coordination was impressive, but more than a little creepy. I glanced away from them.

"Look," Davis said. "I'm online way more than I want to be. If I spent that time practicing, I'd be the best quarterback in the state."

Caitlin leaned against Davis's shoulder. "Recognizing a problem is the first step to fixing it. So do it with us," she suggested. "Turn off social media. We can support each other."

He thought about it for a minute, then clapped his hands together like he was breaking up a huddle. "Let's do it."

Caitlin grinned at him. "Go, Team SO."

He raised his eyebrows in question.

"Stay Offline," I explained.

"I think the name needs work, but okay," he said. "Go, SO." He gave me and then Caitlin a high five. I smiled.

"I'll talk to Ben about it, too," Davis said. "He gets horrible messages on ChitChat. He says it doesn't bother him, but I know it does."

"Cool," I said, surprised. I'd always thought of the vow as just belonging to me, Cait, and Luna. But having Ben and Davis be a part of it felt sort of good, too.

If only I could stop thinking about my phone in my bag. How easy it would be to download ChitChat again and reactivate my account.

Coach Stone blew the whistle out at midfield, then yelled at the defensive linemen to get their heads in the game.

"You'd better get over there," Caitlin said to Davis. "He's going to want the offensive team on the field next."

"What about the kicking team?" Davis asked. "You need the practice, too."

"We all know he's not going to let me actually play," Caitlin said. "I'm not even going to step foot on that field."

"You don't give him enough credit," Davis said.

Caitlin sighed. "You're right. I should be more grateful."

Davis smiled at her. "And grateful for SO. It's going to make us even better."

He picked up his helmet and jogged out toward the field.

My phone buzzed in my bag with a text. I'd long since moved past thinking any incoming texts were from Jameson. I pulled out my phone to see a text from my mom, saying I needed to be home for dinner.

I told Caitlin I had to go, gave her a quick good-luck hug, and then headed up through the bleachers to get to the parking lot.

On my way, I passed by Mariah and Jordyn, and tried not to meet their gazes.

"Hey, Annie," Mariah said in a fake-sweet voice. "Are you voting for the Fall Festival band?" she asked me when I walked by. Her perfectly outlined lips formed something that resembled a smile.

The Fall Festival band. Discord. What did she mean about a vote, though? I shrugged, trying to act like I knew what she was talking about.

"The three finalists posted their auditions on ChitChat," Jordyn chimed in. "Discord's song is awesome."

Oh. I'd forgotten that Jameson must have had the audition by now.

Mariah raised an eyebrow at me. The blue glitter on her eyelids sparkled like tinsel on a Christmas tree. "Have you not watched it yet?" she asked. "You know, I haven't seen you on ChitChat in a while."

I blinked, my thoughts racing. She wanted a reaction from me, so I was careful not to give one. I wanted to tell her that I'd gone off ChitChat, that I didn't need the app, and that I didn't need to watch Jameson's audition. But I couldn't speak.

For a moment, our eyes locked, and my throat tightened. The look Mariah gave me froze me. It was unmistakable. *Pity.* There was a squeezing feeling in my stomach. Finally, I turned and walked away.

But I had a horrible feeling that I was going to do something very, very wrong.

⏻   ⏻   ⏻

Later that night, long after dinner, I lay in bed and thought about Mariah, and Jameson, and ChitChat. I thought about the vow. And I tried everything. I tried writing in the notebook. I tried meditating. I wrote a poem. But nothing worked.

I could have texted Luna and Caitlin an SOS, but I knew they were both sleeping by now. Besides, it was also like I *didn't* want their help. I didn't want them to know.

I grabbed my phone.

I'll just look to see what song Discord played, I told myself, my heart racing. *I'll watch the video, and then I'll delete ChitChat again.*

My fingers were trembling as I downloaded the ChitChat app. Before I knew what I was doing, I'd reactivated my account.

I was back on.

I couldn't keep away from my prison. I chose to go back inside and let the door clang shut behind me.

I drank in everything I'd been missing—the photos and the posts and the hashtags. It felt so good at first.

Just watch the song, I told myself sternly. *That's all.*

I clicked over to the student council's page, where the audition videos had been posted, and I pressed play on the Discord video.

Discord's song was one I'd heard many times before. But they sounded better than ever. Jameson not only sounded good, he looked good, too. Ugh.

I checked the votes. Discord was way ahead. I imagined Jameson watching ChitChat with his band, giving high fives all around as the votes climbed higher and higher in their favor. At this rate, it was almost assured Jameson would be up on the Fall Festival stage, playing for the whole school.

I let out a breath. Okay. I'd watched the video. I'd seen the votes. I was done. I should delete the app. I could keep the vow. I would be seeing Luna and Caitlin the next day at the salon. We were dyeing our hair together as a symbol of the vow. I could still face them if I deleted ChitChat now.

My mind screamed at me to go, but I needed to stay. Just a little longer.

I read the comments under the video.

OHHH. LEAD SINGER IS HOT! IS HE AVAILABLE?

NOW HE IS. JAMESON HAS OPTIONS NOW AND A FAT
GIRL AIN'T ONE OF THEM.

I winced. My body was a joke to them. Something to
laugh about and comment on. I clicked over to my own
ChitChat account.

Even though *I'd* been gone, and even though there
were way fewer new comments now, a couple trolls had
stuck around, still snarking on some of my photos.

Reality morphed and shifted into a handheld screen
full of anonymous voices. If they said the grass was purple
and the sky was green, I would never know the difference as long as I stayed right here looking at my phone.
All I needed to know was here in my hand. Why go anywhere else? The voices told me what music to listen to,
what clothes to wear, what my face should look like, what
my body should look like.

At any moment, I could have walked out of this prison.
But I stayed.

And scrolled.

And my world reshaped to the truth they wanted me
to believe.

If only I had brown eyes
If only I had straight hair
If only I was thin
If only I was tall
If only I was shorter
If only I was smarter
If only I was cooler
I would be perfect.

Annie

⏻　⏻　⏻

Hey, you,

　　Today I am going to write you (I mean me) a poem. It's one of the things on the list for me to check off and since I don't have to show anyone, it doesn't really matter what I say, right?

　　Missing you
　　Is what I do
　　Don't show it
　　Don't blow it

I know. I know. I would make a terrible Dr. Seuss.

Cait

⏻ ⏻ ⏻

Today I talked to my grandmother on the phone. It's been a while. Longer than it should have been. The list reminded me.

She spoke in Spanish and sometimes I didn't understand, even though I tried to hide it as best I could. I didn't want her to know I lost words. They slipped out of my brain when I wasn't listening hard enough. When she lived with us, I never thought about how to talk. It just happened. Spanish. English. My brain moved seamlessly between the two. One sentence in one. One sentence in the other.

I told her I would call her again next week. I can't forget.

Te amo, Abuela.

Luna

CHAPTER FOURTEEN

The whole point is to live life and be—to use all the colors in the crayon box.

—RuPaul

"Have you girls figured out the shade you want?"

The hairstylist, Taylor, had spiky purple hair and thick eyelash extensions that made it look like an effort to blink. She wore a black holster belt filled with scissors and combs and stood with her hands on her hips, waiting for my friends and me to decide.

It was Saturday, and Caitlin, Luna, and I were sitting on a bench near the salon entrance. I still felt awful about my slipup last night, but in the light of day, it no longer felt quite so serious. After scrolling for a while, I *had* found the strength to delete the app again, and I'd fallen asleep quickly. I figured there was no need to tell my friends about what had happened. It was just a one-time thing.

Caitlin fingered the swatches of color in her hands, looking doubtful. I was sure she was thinking of the reaction she was going to get when she showed up on the field with pink hair. Her dad would be surprised. Or maybe even angry. I could tell she was having second thoughts.

She took a breath, probably about to admit it, when I pointed decisively to the brightest pink at the end of the row of color swaths.

"This one," I said.

Luna nodded in agreement. "Yes, that's perfect."

We both looked at Caitlin expectantly. She swallowed hard, then finally agreed.

Taylor smiled. "I love that shade of pink."

"But it's not permanent, right?" Caitlin asked. She stood up and paced restlessly in front of the picture windows facing Walnut Street.

Taylor shook her head. "It will only last a few weeks."

Caitlin stopped pacing. I smiled at her encouragingly.

My friends and I got up and settled into three side-by-side salon chairs while Taylor mixed and stirred creams into a bowl.

I looked at my friends in the mirror and saw that Luna was frowning. "Are you worried about the pink hair, too?" I asked her.

Luna shook her head. "The newspaper. The story I was chasing yesterday went nowhere. I have to come up with *something* or there's no way I'll be chosen as the new editor in chief."

"Don't worry. It's going to be okay," Caitlin said.

"Is it?" Luna asked.

"Have you done anything else off the list?" I asked Luna, to take her mind off the editor in chief thing.

"I organized my closet, so we can check that one off,"

Luna said with a smirk. "It was probably a way to avoid working on my English essay, but now all my shirts are color coded."

"Just shirts?" Caitlin asked.

"It's a start," Luna pointed out.

"Well, good for you," I said, "because I definitely wasn't going to do that one."

"Neither was I," Caitlin admitted.

An assistant flung capes over our shoulders and clipped towels tightly around our necks. This was definitely happening. Whether I was ready or not. The three of us sitting there would have made a great ChitChat photo. #changeiscoming #newdo #makeover

Taylor interrupted my thoughts. "Who wants to go first?" she asked.

Caitlin and Luna looked surprised when I spoke up. "I do."

"Okay." Taylor stood with her brush at the ready. "All over? Or just a stripe?"

"Here," I said, pulling out a swath of my blond hair from the left side. ChitChat trolls immediately screamed in my ear in response.

WHAT WAS SHE THINKING?

IS SHE SUPPOSED TO BE A PINK SKUNK?

SRSLY??? NOBODY DOES THAT ON PURPOSE.

SHE THINKS IF WE'RE LOOKING AT THAT HAIR, WE'LL
FORGET ABOUT THE BODY.

I tried to ignore the words in my brain and sucked in my breath as Taylor coated the strip of hair with a thick paste, then wrapped it up in tinfoil.

Luna went next, choosing a piece from right under her ear. "When I tuck my hair behind my ears, it'll show up perfectly," she said, and Taylor enthusiastically agreed.

Caitlin shifted in her chair, tapping her Frye moto boots restlessly against the metal footrests of the salon chair.

"And finally . . ." Taylor stood in front of Caitlin, holding the bowl in one hand and the brush in the other.

"Put it back here," Caitlin said. She pulled her hair up off her neck, leaving a small section behind that hung down between her shoulders. With her hair down or tucked up in a helmet, no one would even know the pink was there. She glanced nervously at me, then explained, "I don't know if my dad would approve."

I considered, then said, "I think it will look great."

Caitlin breathed a sigh of relief.

After all the creams and foils were applied, the three of us sat in our chairs waiting for the magic to happen. A now-familiar unease settled into my stomach. I glanced around. We were the only ones without phones in our hands. My phone was a filler for blank spaces. Until the vow, I never noticed how much space there was I didn't know how to fill.

Waiting in a line.

Chewing.

Riding in a car.

Waiting for hair to turn pink.

Luna noticed it, too. "Even when I think I've gotten used to it, I still feel like I should be on ChitChat all the time."

The memory of what I'd done last night came back with a snap. I sat up tall and reminded myself to breathe.

"Davis and Ben want to take the vow," Caitlin said, spinning herself slowly round and round in the chair. "Annie and I mentioned it to Davis at practice last night, and he was interested. Is that cool with you?" she asked Luna.

"Of course," Luna said. "What made them want to get off social media?" She slid toward the edge of her chair. She had a suppressed kind of energy about her. I knew that look. Luna's brain was suddenly starting to buzz.

"They just wanted a break from all the judgment. Same as us, I guess," Caitlin said. "What's wrong? I shouldn't have shared?"

"No, you absolutely should have shared!" Luna exclaimed. She was practically quivering with excitement. "In fact, I think we need to share it with everyone."

I felt a twinge of worry. What did Luna mean? The vow wasn't supposed to be about everyone. It was just about us, right?

Caitlin looked at Luna like the hair dye might be seeping a little too deeply into her brain.

"Don't you see?" Luna stood up suddenly, her plastic

cape billowing behind her like she was a superhero of the salon. "This is the perfect story. It's about what happens when kids turn off their screens and live their real lives."

Caitlin blinked, her brows furrowed. "Go on."

"Kids who want to participate in the offline vow turn off their social media for one month," Luna said. "I could follow some of the participants and tell their stories."

"Wait a minute," I said, understanding now. "You want this to be your news story?"

Luna snapped her fingers, then pointed at me excitedly. "Exactly." Her eyes were sparkling. "This vow thing could be so much bigger than just us. What if people sign their name to the vow publicly so they have to be accountable for their promise? Others see it and realize social media is a negative influence in their lives, too. And it takes off . . . like a snowball rolling downhill."

"Overused simile," Caitlin said teasingly.

"Okay," Luna said, smiling. "It takes off . . . like a viral cat meme."

"Better." Caitlin laughed.

"Or a wildfire," I said, but I wasn't laughing.

What did all this mean? Luna was going to *write* about our vow? And she wanted more people to be a part of it? Suddenly it felt like things were happening too fast.

And what about the fact that I'd broken the vow last night? Should I share my secret with my friends now, before we got too many other people involved? But Luna's face was flushed with triumph, so I swallowed down my uncertainty and didn't say anything more.

"Yes, a wildfire," Luna said, her eyes alert. "I like that."

"You have to light the spark first," Caitlin said. "Do you know how you're going to kick this thing off?"

"Not yet," Luna admitted. "But it's going to have to be big."

CHAPTER FIFTEEN

One's destination is never a place but rather a new way of looking at things.

—Henry Miller

Early Monday morning, way before breakfast time, Luna texted me and Caitlin to meet her at school before the bell. She said she was ready to put her plan into action. Caitlin texted back that she had morning football practice, but that we should fill her in on everything later. I told Luna I'd meet her at school.

Slipping out of bed, I headed for the shower. I felt guilty and tired. I had failed again last night and logged back on to ChitChat. I told myself I would only look at faraway places. Like Paris. But of course that had turned into more endless scrolling until finally I'd managed to pull myself out of the hole and delete the app again.

Just breathe.

It was too early to eat breakfast and I felt way too anxious to even consider it. When I arrived at school, the hallways were deserted except for Luna standing right in the middle of the foyer with a huge grin on her face. She pulled out the stack of flyers and a roll of tape from her backpack. She handed me a pile of the neon-yellow papers and I read with trepidation.

DO YOU FEEL TRAPPED IN A SOCIAL MEDIA WORLD?

IS LIFE PASSING YOU BY WHILE YOU'RE ON
THE PHONE?

LIVE YOUR LIFE—DON'T JUST POST ABOUT IT.

JOIN US FOR THE #OFFLINEOCTOBER CHALLENGE!

MEET US AT MUGS THIS WEDNESDAY AT
4 P.M. TO LEARN MORE!

The guilt stabbed my heart. "Wow," I said. "You're really going for it."

"Yep." Luna spread her arms and looked over her shoulder. I followed her gaze.

She had been busy. There were neon-yellow signs on every single door of every single classroom. On lockers. On the library windows. It was impressive. Even for Luna.

"It's sad, but I really want to take a picture of all my hard work and post it on ChitChat," she said with a laugh. "I guess it's hardwired into our brains."

I nodded, chewing on my lower lip.

Tell her you broke the vow.

She looked so happy. So excited. I couldn't ruin it. Not now.

"Do you think people will want to take part in this?" I asked her carefully.

Luna nodded. "Definitely. People will be intrigued, at least. It's like an invitation to an exclusive club." She looked at me and added, "You can be there at Mugs on Wednesday afternoon, right? Caitlin already said she can come. I can't do this without the two of you."

My stomach clenched. I didn't want to be part of a group project. When I finally got up the nerve to tell Luna and Caitlin that I'd gone on ChitChat, they would understand. Or at least I hoped they would. But if more and more kids were part of the vow? There was no way I wanted my failure to somehow become another public spectacle.

But how could I say no to Luna after all she'd done for me? "Sure, I'll be there," I said. It was the least I could do, considering my betrayal.

"Great. Can you put the rest of these up by the front entrance?" Luna asked me, handing me a roll of tape. "You're taller than me, so maybe you can hang one up right over the door?"

"I'll try," I said. I went over to the entrance, but I wasn't quite tall enough to reach above the door. So I found a stepladder to borrow in the janitor's closet and stood on it, stretching my arms up with the flyer in hand. It was still hard to reach. Time was ticking. Students would pour into those front doors at any minute, and I was sure Luna wanted everything ready by then.

"Do you want some help with that?" I heard a voice behind me ask.

I turned carefully on the stepladder to see Isco standing there, an amused half smile on his face. I flushed. I hadn't seen him at school since the day I met him at the animal shelter. Since we'd had that somewhat awkward encounter with the jumper cables. But I had learned that his full name was Francisco Rizal, and he was a senior.

I didn't want Isco to think I was some damsel in distress, always in need of saving. But at the same time, he *was* taller than me and could probably get the flyer up there without any trouble.

"Okay," I finally said.

He sauntered over and joined me on the stepladder. I handed him the flyer and the tape, and he posted the flyer quickly, right above the door.

"Thanks," I mumbled.

"No problem," he said. He read over the sign, his eyes bright with interest. "This sounds cool. Are you involved in it?"

I shrugged. "Sort of."

I climbed down from the stepladder, and Isco followed. "Hey," he said. "I'm working at the shelter after school today. Maybe I'll see you there?"

"Maybe," I said. I realized that going to the shelter would help keep me away from ChitChat. I waved to Isco and hurried off to return the stepladder to the janitor's closet.

The halls were full of students by then. I heard someone say, "Cool hair."

I turned and saw Tiffany Grimes, who sat next to me in English class. She smiled, opening her locker.

I ran my fingers through my hair nervously. "You think so?"

"Absolutely."

"Thanks," I said, feeling surprised. I'd only been expecting snide remarks on my hair, but Tiffany's kindness gave me a boost.

After I returned the stepladder to the janitor's closet, I went to rejoin Luna by her locker.

Luna was chatting excitedly with Ms. Spencer, the journalism teacher and newspaper advisor. I liked Ms. Spencer. She wore hardly any makeup, but still looked beautiful with clear brown skin, high cheekbones, and dark curly hair that was usually pulled up into a messy bun on top of her head and fastened with a stray pencil. I thought that looked particularly reporter-like. Just like in old movies. Now reporters would probably have to stick a phone in their hair and that wouldn't look good at all. I especially liked her no-nonsense style of jeans, T-shirts, and sneakers. She looked like she was always ready to run out to a breaking story.

"I think this has all the makings of a great story," I heard Ms. Spencer saying to Luna. She tapped the flyer Luna had handed to her. "As I like to say, anything can be news, but not everything is newsworthy."

I saw the burst of pride on Luna's face. "Thank you," she said, but I could tell she wanted to say so much more.

Praise from Ms. Spencer was hard to get, and that made it even more special.

Ms. Spencer's tiny, all-knowing smile told me she knew exactly how much this compliment meant to Luna.

"I'll let Tamar know you're working on this piece," Ms. Spencer said. "I'm sure she'll be quite impressed." She gave Luna a meaningful look, and I felt my heart jump. Did that mean Ms. Spencer thought Tamar might like this idea enough to make Luna the new editor in chief?

Luna's eyes were sparkling. "I hope so," she said. Suddenly, she caught my hand and held it. "The idea wouldn't even exist without Annie," she told Ms. Spencer proudly. "Her story is the most inspiring part of this whole offline challenge."

The trust in her voice made my heart skip.

If only she knew.

○   ○   ○

After school, I went back to the shelter, and Isco didn't seem surprised at all to see me. He printed my name on a blank name tag without even a reminder. Looking at the top of his head bent over the desk, I noticed how his hair was thick and dark and shiny. Then I kicked myself for noticing. Cute boys with good hair and big smiles only brought heartache. And I didn't need any more of that.

When Isco finished writing, his pen rolled across the desk, and I reached for it, tipping over a potted plant in the process. I froze in horror as dirt spilled across the desk and onto the tiled white floor. I sank down onto my knees, scooping up the dirt with my hands and dumping huge handfuls back into the now-upright pot.

"I . . . That's not necessary." Isco peered at me over the top of the desk.

"I'm so sorry." I kept working, flinging dirt desperately in the general direction of the pot, feeling the heat of embarrassment engulf my face. I wasn't sure if I was sorry about the mess I'd made here, or the mess I was making by breaking the vow and not telling my friends.

Isco walked around the desk and reached for my dirty hands, making me stop. "Seriously, Annie. It's no big deal. I'll clean this up with the broom."

I pulled my hands out of his grasp and wiped them on the back of my jeans. "Thanks," I said. "I've had better days."

"But you're here now, so you can leave all the bad stuff out there," he said, motioning toward the parking lot. "Do you want a new assignment?"

I shook my head. "I brought something for Rocco."

"I like the pink streak," he told me as he led me down the hall to Rocco's kennel. "It suits you."

"Oh," I said, blushing. "Thanks." I hadn't blushed when Tiffany—and a couple other kids at school—had complimented my hair today. I shook my head, annoyed at myself.

Rocco seemed to recognize me immediately, picking up his head and immediately trotting over to the gate with his tail wagging enthusiastically. He sat down and pushed his soft brown snout through the opening for a scratch.

I stroked his nose, then squatted down to meet his eyes, crooning through the fence. "Hi, sweetie."

Rocco's tail waved even faster, thumping rhythmically on the concrete floor.

Isco smiled. "It's okay if you read to him inside the kennel, but only if you're comfortable. Give him some extra time and attention. Give him a chance. He needs you."

And maybe I need him, too, I thought.

Isco headed back out to the front, and I settled down on the floor beside the gate and pulled out a new book. It was a picture book that I'd taken out from the library, about howler monkeys in Costa Rica. Rocco loved the pictures, and I tried to make the sound of the monkeys for him. He tilted his head, perking his ears and listening closely—and I almost thought he was laughing with his big, panting grin.

After a while, I decided it was time. I slipped inside the kennel to sit on the floor next to Rocco and read the book to him again. Small excited yips escaped his mouth every time I turned the page to a new picture.

After we were done, I stroked his soft nose, and he rested his head on top of my thigh. His breathing was deep and measured against my leg. I matched my breaths to his, feeling my heartbeat steady and slow. It was hard to believe a dog could express such different emotions. Right above his eyes were these movable bones—sort of like doggy eyebrows. When he was excited, they went up, and when his head was resting on my leg, his doggy eyebrows pulled down tight in concentration like he was listening intently to anything I might want to say. So I started talking.

"Someday I'm going to Costa Rica," I told Rocco. He looked at me like he totally believed it. I chewed on the nail of my pinkie and told Rocco how I dreamed of jungles, beaches, cliffs, and sunsets.

"That's almost what I've been missing most about ChitChat," I explained. "The travel pictures. I love looking at them. Even now." I stroked Rocco's soft brown nose. "I don't think that's such a bad part of social media, is it?"

His tail thumped hard against the concrete in response.

I squirmed around on the concrete, then frowned down at Rocco. "It's pretty bad that I'm breaking the vow, huh? But I won't tell anyone if you won't."

Rocco rolled his brown eyes up to meet mine. No judgment.

When your dad is bigger than life, you can't help but be smaller. I don't want to keep fighting to get above the water, but I think sometimes I'm drowning from all the attention heaped on him. Maybe that's why I keep trying to do something people say I can't? Iain McCloud is the huge center on the team. Anyway, he told me the other day at practice that he collects erasers. I asked him why and he said because he makes a lot of mistakes. The erasers make him feel like things are fixable. I liked that.

Cait

CHAPTER SIXTEEN

Isn't everyone a part of everyone else?

—Budd Schulberg

On Wednesday afternoon at 4:00 p.m., Luna, Caitlin, and I gathered at Mugs to wait for others to join us for #OfflineOctober—or not. Luna had reserved a big table in the back and ordered the three of us our favorite drinks.

"Who do you think is coming?" Caitlin asked, sipping her latte.

"I'm not sure. There's really no way to know," Luna said. She pulled out her laptop and powered it up. "Only a few people told me they would be here, but hopefully word has spread more."

Ever since Luna had put up the flyers, there'd been buzz throughout the hallways about "Offline October" and what it meant.

"If Mariah shows up, I'm leaving," I said firmly.

"Me too," Caitlin said.

"I don't think she'll be here," Luna said. "It's not her style to give up ChitChat for one day, much less a month."

Just then, the door opened and Isco walked in. My eyes widened.

"What are you doing here?" I asked as he approached

our table. He wore a faded blue T-shirt with an unzipped gray hoodie.

"I like coffee. I hear they sell it here." He flashed me his big smile. "Besides, you know, I *did* see this flyer about a meeting here today. Thought I'd check it out."

I couldn't help but smile back, even though I was a little flustered to have him here.

"Welcome," Luna said, gesturing to an open seat at the long table. "I'm Luna, by the way. This is Caitlin, and that's Annie."

Isco nodded. "Nice to meet you all. I'm Isco. Annie and I work together at the shelter."

That made Caitlin look up from her drink. "What shelter?"

"Um," I said. "I've been volunteering at the animal shelter . . . That was the thing I picked to do off the list."

"Really?" Luna said with a *this is all very interesting* look on her face. I could tell she was dying to ask me why I hadn't mentioned the shelter, or Isco.

I was relieved when two freshman girls came into the café and walked over to our table.

I recognized them mostly from their fashionista posts online, although I didn't know them well. One wore a slouchy pink sweater over black leggings tucked into leopard-skin booties. The other paired her black Doc Martens boots with a white tank tucked into a daisy-patterned midi skirt. They sat whispering to each other in the chairs at the end of the table while Isco went to get coffee.

More people started to trickle in. Thankfully, there were no signs of Mariah, Jordyn, Jameson, or Milo. Davis and his boyfriend, Ben, showed up and sat down near Caitlin. Then a girl I didn't recognize walked in. She was overweight, dressed all in black with thick black eyeliner, and wore deep purple eye shadow. The girl sat down in the chair beside the wall and looked like she wanted to disappear. My heart went out to her. I felt like she would get me.

"Hey. My name is Annie," I said to her.

The girl nodded, then mumbled, "Jennifer."

"Welcome," I said.

Isco came back with his coffee. Now there was a total of nine kids settled self-consciously around the table. I looked around the group, curious. *Why would each of them want to leave ChitChat?* Maybe they needed this break from their own self-consciousness and self-obsession just as much as I did.

I could tell Luna was ecstatic with the turnout. Her brown eyes were gleaming. Sure, Luna could write the article about just the three of us taking the vow, but that wouldn't be good enough. Not for Luna. This story needed to be bigger. And this group of teenagers—all wide-eyed and uncomfortable—was just what she'd been looking for.

Luna stood up from her chair. "I want to thank everyone for coming. You are all interested in the offline challenge, yes?"

Most nodded. A few shrugged.

Luna continued. "I'm going to be documenting our journey for our school newspaper and I'd like to know a little more about why you're taking the vow to leave ChitChat."

The two fashionistas were already glancing to the side, knees jittering nervously up and down. One was chewing on a fingernail. The other looked like she was counting ceiling tiles. And then there was Caitlin, who kept clicking the top on her pen in and out and in and out.

Click. Click. Click.

I wanted to post a photo of just the circle of restless hands and feet. I would label it #withdrawal #missingChitChat #OfflineOctober.

"Okay, I'll start," Luna said. She held up her phone. "This," she said, "is like a Wheel of Fortune. Every time you open ChitChat, you spin the wheel. Sometimes you receive a reward—a like, a follow, a message, a comment. Sometimes you don't, but the times you do are enough to trigger a chemical reaction in your brain. So you come back again. And again. And again."

"Like rats in an experiment?" Davis asked, wrinkling his nose.

Luna leaned forward and nodded. "Exactly. Your brain releases an actual chemical called dopamine." Unsurprisingly, Luna had done her research. "That burst of dopamine makes your brain want to repeat whatever it was you did to give you that good feeling," she went on.

"It's the same chemical that's released in your body when you exercise or eat something delicious or have a successful social interaction."

"Like falling in love?" I asked. I noticed Isco glance my way, and I tried to keep my gaze on Luna.

She nodded. "Yep."

"So we all need to, I don't know, fall in love or eat chocolate or run around the block a few times instead," Caitlin said, matter-of-fact.

"Or we could just have more successful real-life interactions, right?" Jennifer spoke up from the corner.

"We could, but think about this. You interact in person with maybe a hundred and fifty people total, but this . . ." Luna waved the smartphone at the group. "This device allows you to increase that to a potential of over four *billion* people. All capable of giving you that jolt of dopamine."

Cait frowned. "Even I couldn't run that much."

"I know some of you have already committed to the vow. So how is it going so far?" Luna asked. She sat back down, ready to take notes on her computer.

There was an awkward pause, but Luna let it go on until finally one of the fashionista freshmen broke the silence.

"Okay, I'll go. My name is Kiyana." She gave a half wave to the group. A few waved back, some just smiled. "I've only been off ChitChat for one day, and it's been super tough for me. Much harder than I thought it would be. I feel anxious. I'm scared I'm missing out on everything. I used to know what people were doing and where they were."

"Were you invited to go do things with them before?" Luna asked, typing furiously.

"No. I just saw it on ChitChat." She shook her head. "I know. Saying it aloud makes me realize how silly it sounds. But that's how I feel."

Davis spoke up. "It's not silly. I feel that way, too." He looked around the faces, meeting eyes. "I bet a lot of people here do."

A few nodded, obviously surprised by the superstar quarterback's admission.

"So how did that make you feel when you saw on ChitChat they were excluding you?" Luna asked, typing away.

"Not great," Kiyana said. "But I *knew* about it. Now they are still excluding me and I don't even know about all the amazing things they are doing."

"Which is worse?" Jennifer asked from the corner. "Having imaginary online friends or no friends at all?"

Everyone looked at her, but no one answered the question.

"It's not just about being left out," Ben said. "It feels so isolating. Like I can't share even the good things with anyone. I used to have . . . like, an audience. Now nothing."

The other fashionista with the pink sweater sighed. "Exactly."

"I get these nasty comments sometimes," Ben said. "Most of the time they're from random cowards who don't even know me. I try to ignore them, but they get into my head, you know?" He looked around the circle.

More nods.

"I get that, of course," I told Ben.

But of course I'm also back on social media, I thought. *Nobody here knows that I'm a liar.*

Guilt made my eyes sting. I blinked hard.

"When you are on social media, do you feel supported?" Luna asked the group.

Caitlin shook her head. "I feel competition. But it's like a game where I don't know the rules and I can't win no matter what I do."

Several people nodded.

"This isn't easy for any of us," Luna said. "We're happy to have you all decide to try this with us."

"Don't get me wrong. I think the offline vow sounds great and all," I said, twisting a strand of my hair around my finger like I always did when I was thinking hard. "But how do we know we'll actually keep our promise?"

Because I'm not.

"Of course we'll keep our promise!" Caitlin leaned into the circle to drape her arms around each of the shoulders next to her. Now was the time to inspire teamwork. "We're *us*."

"If we're really going to do this, we need some accountability," Luna said.

Isco looked around the circle of faces. "I agree. We have to do something public. Something that holds us accountable to everyone, not just to each other."

"Maybe we don't have to tell the whole world," I said. "Maybe we can just tell each other."

I glanced away and accidentally looked right at Isco. He offered his usual half smile, but I looked away quickly, not wanting him to see my panic. I squared my shoulders and focused back on the brainstorming session. I felt my teeth clench but managed a smile just in case he was still watching.

"No," Caitlin said abruptly. "We need something very public."

The faces around the circle got much more serious. The stakes were suddenly higher, and the only sound was the murmur of conversations in the rest of the room and the occasional rattle of the blender.

"I know." Caitlin snapped her fingers excitedly. "We sign our names to a poster by the office and everyone in school sees it."

"That's good!" Isco said, and Luna started typing.

I could see Luna's brain buzzing with possibilities. "Once we all make a public declaration, maybe other people will want to join us. And then . . . we do some kind of big gesture to recognize participants." Her eyes gleamed with excitement. This was definitely the story she'd been looking for, the one that would get her the editor position. "It could take over the whole school."

Ben jumped in. "The Fall Festival," he said firmly. "That's the place. Maybe it's a ceremony, and we give out certificates to everyone who kept the vow?"

I kept my face neutral. Jameson was singing at the Fall Festival and I was determined to not be anywhere near that stage when it happened.

"I love that idea!" Luna said.

Lizzie, the other freshman fashionista, frowned. "There's only about two weeks from now until the Fall Festival and the vow is supposed to be for a month, right?"

"So maybe everyone just vows to stay offline until the Fall Festival. Even if it's only a couple weeks instead of a full month," her friend suggested.

"Good." Luna nodded. "The Fall Festival will be perfect. I can even bring Annie and Caitlin up to talk about the month-long commitment to give a sense of what's possible."

She looked around expectantly, and the group smiled back at her, nodding. Everyone but me. I felt the rapid beat of my heart. Now I was going to be a liar in front of the whole school, not just to my best friends. I glanced over at Isco. He was still watching me, leaning back in his chair now like he was at the movie theater. It was obvious he was enjoying the show.

"Maybe that will inspire some to continue after the Fall Festival," Davis said.

Ben nodded. "At least it will give everyone a chance to try it out even if it's only for two weeks."

"Two weeks is a long time," Caitlin said.

No one said anything. They were obviously thinking about how difficult it had been for just a few days.

"The list," Luna said. "We can all pick an activity to do together."

"Like what?" Davis asked.

Luna pulled up the list on her computer and began to read aloud.

"Wait," Ben said, pointing at her. "Let's do that one— be a tourist in your own town. I heard of the ghost tour they have in Old Town and I've always wanted to go. Let's all do it together tomorrow night."

Davis nodded. "I'm in."

Heads nodded around the circle. Being together might actually help us all.

I spoke up suddenly, breaking the silence. "If people ask us why we are doing all this, what do we say? What's the point?"

Jennifer looked around the group slowly, meeting the eyes of each person in turn. "To be happier," she said quietly.

CHAPTER SEVENTEEN

Our feet are planted in the real world, but we dance with angels and ghosts.

—John Cameron Mitchell

The man in the black top hat and red cape stood in the doorway just off the square. The chalkboard beside him said that the next tour would start in ten minutes, so I knew I was in the right place, even if no one else from Team SO had shown up yet.

The evening air was crisp, and I was glad for the blue jean jacket I'd pulled off the coatrack when I left home. Not sure of the appropriate attire for ghost hunting, I'd decided comfort was critical. I wore soft fleece-lined leggings under tall leather riding boots, a gray sweater, and a red scarf bright enough to hopefully scare away the dead.

"Boo."

I turned to see Isco standing behind me wearing jeans and a black hoodie.

"Hey," I said, caught a little off guard. But then I smiled, glad he was here. He gave me one of his brilliant smiles back.

Luna came around the corner, trailed by Davis and Ben. She wore a simple white tee and jeans, topped off by an ankle-grazing sweater duster and a black camera strapped to her chest.

"What are you going to do with that?" I pointed to the camera.

Luna shrugged. "Well, I didn't want to bring my *phone* . . . but I need to document our group's first real outing for my story."

I nodded. Right. The story. I felt a flash of guilt, thinking of my phone tucked away in my crossbody bag. At least it was turned off.

"Anyone else coming from Team SO?" I asked. Caitlin had opted out of tonight's choice of activity, saying ghosts really weren't her thing. Jennifer had said it was her sister's birthday, and there was a family dinner she had to attend. I wasn't sure about the two freshman fashionistas.

Davis shook his head. "Lizzie and Kiyana had plans, but they promised it didn't involve anything online."

"So I guess it's just us," Isco said.

A middle-aged couple walked over to join the ghost tour. The man was no taller than my chest and had a long, thin ponytail that almost reached his waist. His companion, a woman, was much taller than him and spoke in a heavy accent that I thought might be Swedish. Or German. I couldn't tell.

The guide with the top hat looked around and then down at the list in his hand. "I think we're waiting on two more people." He had a slight British accent, but I thought it might be part of his act.

"Sorry we're late." A man holding a little kid by the hand approached the group. The boy was about six or seven and happily finishing an ice cream cone from the Ben & Jerry's across the square. I shot him a quick smile.

"No worries. We're just ready to leave now." Top Hat Man introduced himself as Jeeves, and I couldn't help but roll my eyes. The British accent was definitely fake. "If you'll all follow me this way, our first stop is just around the corner."

The man with the ponytail and his companion were eager. They stepped into line right beside Jeeves and began asking all sorts of questions about the town. Obviously tourists. The father and son were the next to follow, the man trying to wipe off leftover chocolate from the boy's cheeks with the hem of his shirt while they walked.

"Hey, Annie!" Luna called to me from the back of the line. "Over here."

I turned just in time as she clicked a picture with her camera. I scowled at her, but she said, "I have to document the beginning of our tour, right?"

I sighed. At least I knew the picture wouldn't wind up on ChitChat.

"Do you even know how to use that thing?" Davis asked Luna, nodding toward the camera.

She shrugged. "How hard can it be?"

"I think there are a lot of photographers in this world that would disagree with you," Davis said with a grin.

I glanced around and quickly realized the purpose of Jeeves's tall hat as I saw it disappear around the Starbucks on the corner. It was the only thing that stood out in the crowd of people.

"Come on." I tugged at Isco's arm. "We're going to be lost before we even get to the first stop."

We caught up just as Jeeves disappeared inside a campus apparel shop. I followed the small procession through the bright green pom-poms and racks of T-shirts featuring ram heads, the local university's mascot.

"Have you ever been in here?" I turned to ask Isco.

He shook his head. "But if I knew it was haunted, I would have come."

"It's not haunted," I said firmly. I didn't believe in ghosts, even though the idea did leave me with a tingle of excitement.

"Did you know that in a recent poll, forty-five percent of the people interviewed believed in ghosts?" Luna asked, obviously enjoying himself. "Thirty-two percent even think ghosts can hurt living people."

"How do you know that?" Ben asked.

She shrugged. "I do all kinds of research for stories. Some of it sticks around."

Jeeves stopped at an open space near the back of the store and waited for the group to gather around him. He waved his gold-tipped cane theatrically, gesturing toward the ceiling. Everyone looked up, and I sucked in my breath. The ceiling was a huge stained-glass dome of brilliant greens and blues. Definitely from a different time.

"We're lucky the renovators of the Avery Building decided to keep this beautiful ceiling intact," Jeeves said. "The fascinating part is that it is an acoustic marvel. If you stand in the center"—Jeeves motioned—"and whisper, you can hear the sound all through the room. Go ahead and give it a try."

The little boy went first. "Captain America," he whispered, and we all marveled at how clearly the sound traveled.

"Cool," Isco said to me in a low voice. "But we are here for the ghosts."

Jeeves hadn't heard him, but he did launch into the ghost story then.

"The ghost that inhabits this building," Jeeves announced dramatically, "is named Clark."

Clark? Isco mouthed at me, and I bit my lip to keep from laughing. I knew we were both thinking that "Clark" wasn't a very ghostly sounding name. I felt a strange sense of connection to Isco then, and I glanced away. I looked back at Luna, Ben, and Davis, who were cracking up, too. I held a finger up to my mouth to shush them.

"He was fired from the bank next door and died soon afterward of mysterious circumstances," Jeeves went on, ignoring our antics. The tourist couple and the dad and son hung on to his every word. "Right after this store opened, employees often reported hearing music turning on, lights flickering, and doors slamming when no one was present. One cashier even tells the story of looking up to see a man standing under the dome here, right about closing time. But when she walked over to see if he needed help, he disappeared."

"Duh duh duh." Isco added the musical notes to the end of the story in dramatic fashion, and I smiled, elbowing him in the side. Even though the story was silly, I couldn't help but feel a *little* creeped out.

The tour moved on to the Museum of Art next. Jeeves explained that it was built on top of an 1860s cemetery and supposedly haunted by a ghost named George. The guy with the ponytail asked lots of questions about dates and exhibits, then would repeat the answers loudly to the woman he was with although there was no indication she didn't hear the first time. In fact, each time he repeated the answer, she responded, "I heard." It was so annoying that finally I wandered off to the side to take a closer look at a beautiful yellow mask that resembled a fish I saw on a ChitChat travel account.

"Having fun?" Isco said, joining me.

I thought for a moment, then said, "I actually am. I have to confess I didn't know much about the history of our town."

"But you don't have any questions?" He rolled his eyes toward the guy following Jeeves around the room.

I laughed, then covered my mouth with my hand. "I think they've all been answered. What about you? Are you enjoying our field trip?"

"Actually, I'm terribly disappointed," Isco said, and I

looked at him in surprise. "We keep hearing about all these ghosts, but where *are* they? Why haven't we seen any?"

I just shook my head and rolled my eyes. "Maybe some will appear at some point."

"They better," Ben said, walking over to us with Luna at his side.

"Come on. Jeeves is leaving," Davis said, reaching for Ben's hand. He tugged him along, and Luna followed. Isco and I brought up the rear.

The last stop on the tour turned out to be the most surprising. Jeeves held up his hand as we gathered around him on the sidewalk outside Old Firehouse Books.

"You may not know that there is a series of tunnels and rooms right beneath the sidewalk where we are standing," Jeeves said.

We all looked down at the unassuming bricks under our feet.

"Cool," Ben said, and Davis grinned at him.

"If we head inside, we'll find an entrance." Jeeves motioned to Salus, a natural soap shop, behind him. I had passed this store about a million times and even bought coconut bath bombs there for Luna's and Caitlin's Christmas stockings. But I'd never noticed the stairs on the back wall before. Jeeves led everyone over to the top step and flipped on a flashlight that he pulled from his duster coat pocket. "Stay close."

The tourist couple and the dad and son eagerly followed

Jeeves down the steps, and Luna, Ben, and Davis went next, whispering and giggling.

"You first," Isco said, waving a hand to usher me down into the darkness. I headed toward the flashlight's glow, following Luna step by step and feeling Isco close behind. We quickly left the soap smell behind, crowding into a small space in the basement at the bottom of the stairs.

Jeeves reached over and flipped a switch on the wall, illuminating a string of white lights that revealed a narrow stone tunnel. I gasped. It was as though we'd suddenly descended into another place and time. Now *this* was cool.

I shivered. "This is going to give me nightmares," I whispered.

"Same," Isco admitted, but he was grinning.

"Remember that thirty-two percent of people think ghosts can hurt people?" Luna asked.

"You're not helping." I narrowed my eyes at her.

The man with the ponytail gave us a dirty look. "Shhh," he hissed.

I gave him my best *sorry* look, then focused back on Jeeves.

"Where we're standing used to be the town jail." Jeeves motioned to the caved-in wall. "Long ago, the prisoners were marched through the tunnel underground and up to the Silver Grill for breakfast. The guards would chain their shackles to the rail that lines the bar even today, and then march them back through the tunnels to their cells. But they say some prisoners got lost along the way and continue to haunt these tunnels to this day."

Luna caught my eye and grinned. "Thirty-two percent," she whispered.

I shook my head at her but gave another shiver. Even though I didn't believe in ghosts, the tour was fun. And, I realized with a start, I hadn't thought about checking ChitChat once the whole time. Being in the real world felt surprisingly good. The chatter and judgment in my brain was quiet. At least for now.

⏻ ⏻ ⏻

But later that night, I couldn't win. I got out of bed, ignoring the thread of guilt pulling tight at my stomach, and picked up my phone off the desk. Then, just like I'd done the night before, I found myself clicking around on my phone, into a folder hidden inside a folder hidden inside another folder marked STUFF to find my ChitChat app. It was almost like a ritual. Something about keeping it hidden there within reach felt so wrong, but I was in way too deep now. I couldn't give it up, and I couldn't admit it either.

I told myself, as I often did, that I just wanted to look at the photos from my favorite travel influencers. But then, despite my best intentions, I clicked on Jameson's feed. *Just to remind myself.*

His latest photo was one Mariah had tagged him in. He was at some kind of party. I zoomed in on the photo to look at the surroundings, but I didn't recognize anything. I shrugged and kept scrolling.

I tried to ignore the guilt I felt. *Stop. Turn it off. Walk away.*

If I could just do that now, then maybe tomorrow I might wake up feeling clean again. The whole SO Team was making good on their vow to stay off social media. But I didn't stop. My brain crowded with memes, comments, and photos. With every scroll and each click, I lied about being off social media and betrayed my best friends.

You're a liar. You're a hypocrite.

I looked at the clock on my nightstand. While I read and scrolled, another hour passed. I would never get it back.

Look away from the screen. Just for a moment.

Another hour gone. I had to stop, but the more I looked and read, the more I needed just one more jolt of dopamine. Just. One. More.

Just shut it down and turn it off.

Finally, I slammed my phone facedown on my nightstand, my fists clenched to keep from picking it right back up again.

Scroll to not feel . . .
Heartbroken.
Confused.
Alone.
Bored.
Fill up your prison so you never want to leave.
Or feel anything at all.

Annie

⏻　⏻　⏻

My first game of the season is not important. At least
that's what I keep telling myself. Nothing will feel too
different. I'll still be sitting on the bench, watching. Now I'll
just be watching in pads, uniform, and cleats. There isn't even
a reason to put on my helmet, so I just tuck the strip of pink
hair into my collar and wait.

I know some players didn't want me here. It is obvious by
the way they intentionally bump into me on the way to the
water station or stand directly in my path, refusing to move,
when I run out on the field to practice my kickoffs. They are
subtle, but I know it's only because I am the coach's daughter.
It doesn't matter, I tell myself over and over again. It will
only take one good kick to win them over, if I can just get
the opportunity to prove myself.

But patience has never been one of my strengths.

Caitlin

CHAPTER EIGHTEEN

When you have a dream, you've got to grab it and never let go.

—Carol Burnett

On Friday morning, Team SO gathered before the bell rang by Luna's huge sign in the school's front hall. It had been a week of checking things off the list. Davis and Ben picnicked in the school parking lot, even though they called it tailgating. Lizzie and Kiyana hiked up to Greyrock in coordinated Lululemon outfits. And Jennifer impressed everyone by fixing the 3D printer in the technology lab. Even though there were no posts about these activities on ChitChat, slowly the word was getting out, via the occasional text or phone call, or real-time conversations in the cafeteria. Now Luna was ready to go public in a big way.

The big block letters at the top of the sign read I VOW TO STAY OFFLINE and Luna's name was already written below in decisive red marker. Luna stepped away from the list on the wall with a satisfied sigh. She paused, then looked around the group, stopping to catch each person's eye. I looked down at the tile floor beneath my sneakers. Luna was too good at reading my thoughts, and I wasn't going to give her the chance to see my hesitation.

She handed the marker to Caitlin, who practically jumped in front of the poster and scrawled her name proudly below Luna's. I crossed my arms and waited, a hollow smile plastered to my face.

For a minute, I thought about telling someone the truth. Maybe Isco? I glanced over at him, and he was looking right at me. He lifted his water bottle to his mouth and took a long drink. When he finished, he wiped his mouth on the shoulder of his shirt, then offered me the bottle. I shook my head, and he shrugged with a smile. Meanwhile, all the other members of Team SO were happily signing their names. A crowd of other kids had formed around us, murmuring and snapping pictures. Even some teachers stopped to see what was happening, and they didn't break up the growing crowd.

I watched Isco step up to the poster and sign his name. I realized he was committed just the same as everyone else. I couldn't tell him.

Isco held out the red marker toward me, his eyebrows raised. I could feel Luna and Caitlin watching me, too. I felt slightly sick to my stomach. A wave of panic nearly sent me running in the opposite direction.

Just do it. I sucked in a breath and took the marker from Isco. Feeling more like a liar than ever, I stepped up in front of the poster, then quickly wrote my name at the very bottom.

⏻   ⏻   ⏻

That afternoon, our last-period teacher escorted us down the hall to the gym for the pep rally.

Caitlin waited in the hallway for the big announcement, wearing her oversized jersey and jeans just like the rest of the team. I gave her a quick hug when I walked past. This was her first time as part of a pep rally, but she knew the drill from watching it a million times. When Principal Doane called each name, each member of the football team would jog out into the gym to the roar of the crowd and take their place at center court. One of those empty folding chairs out there was for her. The *her* part was historic and completely awesome.

"Good luck," I said, feeling a surge of pride. I looked out the opening to the gym and saw people already pointing phones toward the doorway. Her entrance would definitely be on ChitChat within minutes after it happened. But neither she nor Luna nor I would see it.

Unless I checked ChitChat later.

Which you won't, I told myself firmly. Yes, I'd briefly gone on it last night. But then I deleted it again.

Caitlin put her hand on her chest and pushed down hard like she was having a heart attack. "I'm kind of freaking out."

I rubbed her shoulder. "You can do this."

"This isn't about making some kind of statement," Caitlin said. "I just want to play."

Milo walked over to Caitlin, head cocked to one side. I tensed up. "You okay?" he asked her.

I had not spoken to Milo since he'd posted the horrible Jameson ChitChat video—the one that had started everything. I wasn't about to speak to him now. I turned a shoulder toward him, trying to block his unwanted interruption.

Caitlin nodded, refastening her hair back into a low ponytail and tucking the pink strands tightly underneath.

I frowned. *Like Milo cared if anyone was okay.*

"You're used to all this," Caitlin told him, looking out at the noisy crowd.

He shrugged. "Just remember. They are out there because it beats going to class."

"I've just never seen it from this side," Caitlin said. "I've always been one of . . . them."

"You . . . *we* . . . still are," I told her reassuringly. "Luna and I will be up there cheering you on. You'll definitely hear us screaming when they call out your name." I gave her another quick hug. "And then we'll be cheering you on at the game later. Okay?"

She nodded, still looking like she might throw up at any minute. I followed the crowd through the door, giving her one last thumbs-up over my shoulder.

The gym looked like there had been an explosion of green confetti and glitter. Everything was covered—from the top of the bleachers to the folding chairs out on the court. The room was filled with every category of student in the school, from student council members to physics bowl winners. No one missed the pep rally since it was basically mandated by a shortened schedule.

I brushed the hair back from my eyes and searched

the crowded bleachers for Luna's supportive face. I saw Jameson up a few rows on my right. He was sitting with his Discord bandmates, but when he saw me, he quickly turned away, chewing on his lower lip. It was a sign I knew well. It meant he was worried about something. He did it the first time he asked me out, and he did it the first time I saw him play in front of an audience. I never mentioned it because I didn't want him to be self-conscious. Or maybe I wanted to keep that secret knowledge all to myself.

What is Jameson worried about? More importantly, why should I care?

I hurtled up the bleachers, headed toward Luna, who was waving wildly at me from a third of the way up in the stands. I squeezed into the empty space beside her and crossed my legs, trying to feel a little smaller and a lot more invisible. I waited for my heart to slow.

The scent of roses and patchouli announced Mariah's arrival like the killer fog I saw one time in a horror movie. She came up the aisles, handing out stacks of bright orange flyers. Her family owned a big farm outside town that featured hayrides, corn mazes, and pick-your-own pumpkins. This year, Mariah's family farm would be the location for the Fall Festival and everyone was talking about how, if all the stars aligned just right, it would also be the perfect celebratory night for the district football champions.

I saw Isco slide into the bench three rows down. When he turned around to pass the flyers up the aisle, he caught my eye and smiled at me. It made me feel strange. Almost light-headed.

No. No. Absolutely not.

I accepted the flyer from the person sitting next to me, then passed one to Luna. Fall leaves and pumpkins bordered the orange handout. The big block letters in the center read JOIN US AT THE FALL FESTIVAL FOR A HARVEST DANCE AND COOKOUT! FEATURING MUSIC BY DISCORD!

Last year, I went to the Fall Festival with Jameson. It was one of our first dates, but we were already a post-worthy couple. The #Annson feed was full of the two of us cuddling in front of the fire, decorating pumpkins, and posing with scarecrows. There was even a video of us getting hopelessly lost in the corn maze. Jameson laughed at how I screamed at the fake skeleton that fell down on top of us.

I shook my head to clear the memory. That was a long time ago.

"Did you see Cait?" Luna asked, and I started to answer, but Principal Doane interrupted by tapping at the microphone.

"Can I have your attention?" The microphone made Principal Doane's voice sound authoritative and godlike— in direct contrast to her five-foot height and tiny build. She stretched up on her toes to get her mouth closer and immediately the feedback squeaked loudly, causing everyone to groan and put their hands over their ears in protest. She backed off slightly and cleared her throat, gripping the podium tight with both hands.

"Before we bring the team out, I want to remind everyone about our Fall Festival after next week's championship game. I know we're going to be celebrating the big win . . ." She paused and the crowd cheered. "Our hardworking student council has gone all out this year to put together an amazing party under the stars, so I know you'll want to get your tickets now."

Principal Doane started introducing the team, and I stood up, wired and expectant, so we could celebrate Cait's triumphant entrance. It seemed strange not to be documenting the moment with my phone. Everywhere I looked, phones were out and people were scrolling, posing, and snapping.

And finally there she was. Caitlin ran out onto the court just as Principal Doane announced, "Caitlin Stone!" A roar went up around the gym, and Luna and I screamed and clapped, jumping up and down. There was something thrilling about seeing Caitlin out there for real, not while holding my phone up in front of my face.

Caitlin waved to everyone, beaming. Then she took her seat beside Davis, who squeezed her shoulder. Luna and I sat back down again, catching our breath.

The cheerleaders came out then, led by Ben, to perform the pregame show. Everyone cheered and clapped more, and then we all filed outside to watch the game. I felt a twinge of nervousness for Caitlin, which I soon forgot when Luna spoke to me.

"I want to interview you for my offline story," Luna said as we climbed the bleachers to take our seats.

I felt like a tree had fallen on my head. *Stupid. Stupid. Stupid.* Somehow I hadn't seen this coming.

"Sort of a personal view of how being offline can be healthy. Cool, right?" Luna bounced on her tiptoes, her eyes crinkled by her wide grin.

I sat down on the bench and slid over to make room for Luna. The team warmed up out on the field below, and I could spot Caitlin among them. Should I tell Luna the truth now? About my cheating? Or would it just ruin Caitlin's big night?

Luna nudged me. "Annie? What do you say?"

I shook my head. "I'm not so sure I'm the best person to interview," I finally answered.

"Tamar says good reporters use all their resources and you are my inside source," Luna said earnestly. "People need to hear how you conquered all that negative publicity. It gives others hope."

But I'm a liar.

My heart was slamming. Crashing. I should tell her. Now. But I stayed silent until the feeling passed and my breathing slowed back to a somewhat normal rate. I took a deep breath in and out again. It was going to be okay because I would stop, I told myself. Last night was my last time on ChitChat.

"Yeah," I finally said. "Sounds great."

Luna gave a satisfied little sigh. "Perfect. Thanks, Annie. We can set up a time for the interview next week."

I looked out onto the field, desperate to change the subject. "The game's about to start."

Caitlin swiveled around on the bench and spotted me and Luna in the stands. We stood and gave her four big thumbs-up, cheering loudly. She waved back and then faced the field again.

The game was going great. Davis threw two fantastic passes and Milo scored two touchdowns. I scowled at Milo's victories, even though I knew it was good for the team—and therefore good for Caitlin and her dad. Luna and I held our breath each time Caitlin's dad waved out the kicker for the extra point, even though it always ended up being Eli Vernon, not Caitlin.

By the third quarter, our team was ahead by four touchdowns. The excitement grew as the score climbed. I found myself more gripped by football than I had ever been before. The cheerleaders practiced their harder stunts, and band members played faster. I knew, from what Caitlin had told me and Luna, that the only hope for her to get into the game was if we got far enough ahead that the second string would be allowed to play. Even then, we didn't know if her dad would actually put Caitlin in the game.

At the beginning of the third quarter, the second-string quarterback, Mike Jackson, ran out on the field, fresh and excited to finally get his big break. Within minutes, Mike ran the ball in for another touchdown. Everyone cheered while the opposing team booed. I saw Caitlin look hopefully at her dad and grip her helmet tightly. My heart went out to her. There was still a chance.

Suddenly, Coach Stone turned, his eyes scanning the people on the sideline until he found Caitlin. He waved her over. This was it. She was going in. She pulled her helmet on over her ponytail and ran out onto the field to huddle.

The teams lined up across from each other, and I waited along with everyone else in the stands for the snap. It was like we were all holding our breaths together. Then Caitlin's foot connected, sending the ball sailing through the goalposts.

"Good." The referees held up their arms, Luna and I screamed with joy, and the team raced to congratulate Caitlin on her history-making kick.

CHAPTER NINETEEN

Friends . . . they cherish one another's hopes. They are kind to one another's dreams.

—Henry David Thoreau

Immediately after the game, Luna and I headed for the girls' locker room to find Caitlin and congratulate her. Her one kick had garnered the team an extra precious point. That had been her only moment on the field, but I knew Caitlin was thrilled. And thanks to Milo scoring another touchdown, our team had won the game. On the way to the locker room, Luna bumped into Tamar, who wanted to chat with her about newspaper stuff, so I went to meet Caitlin on my own. Then I stopped.

Milo stood outside the girls' locker room as if he was waiting for someone. He was freshly showered and wore an oversized Denver Broncos jersey and blue jeans. I wanted to turn around and leave, but no—I wanted to be there for Caitlin more than I wanted to avoid Milo. Besides, I'd promised Caitlin we would celebrate after the game with a movie night at my house. I was even going to let her choose the movie.

"Your girl did great tonight," Milo said when he saw me. He held up his phone. "How about I document it for

ChitChat and take a picture of the two of you when Caitlin gets out?"

I shook my head emphatically, putting my hands up in front of my face. "Stop it, Milo. That's not funny."

"Sorry." He slid the phone into his back pocket. "I didn't mean to upset you. Honestly."

This was the same guy who helped break my heart. He was cruel. But I knew that Caitlin needed his support if she was ever going to be truly accepted by the team. I glanced toward the entrance to the girls' locker room and silently begged her to hurry up. The less time I spent around Milo, the better. I clenched my hands into fists, feeling my nails dig into my palms.

Finally, I glanced back at Milo. I couldn't help myself.

"Why did you post that video of Jameson?" I burst out.

Milo's smile disappeared, but he didn't seem surprised by the question. It was almost like he'd been waiting for it.

"I was tired of him telling me things he needed to tell you. I forced his hand," he said. "I don't like dishonesty."

"It wasn't your place," I snapped.

"I know. You're right," he said. "I thought it would be like ripping a Band-Aid off. Painful, but at least it'd be over."

"But why do it on ChitChat?" I demanded.

Milo looked guilty or unhappy. I couldn't tell which.

"I don't feel good about it," he said. "If I could take it back, I would."

"There are no takebacks on the internet. If it's posted, it never goes away."

He shrugged. "Maybe I need to get away from the social media thing for a while. You know . . . like your vow thing says."

I scowled. "So now you want to leave ChitChat? After all that you did?"

Unbelievable. Milo loved attention. He lived to trade secrets and share gossip. There was no way he was giving up ChitChat.

My face must have given my opinion away, because he swallowed hard and looked sheepish.

"I—I just think it could be a good idea. ChitChat can be toxic. I might consider doing the vow thing, too." He watched me like he was worried. "If it's okay with you."

"Why would I care?" I finally shot back. But I did. I didn't want Milo a part of anything close to me. Plus, a little voice in my head reminded me that I hadn't even been keeping the vow. So what kind of example was there to follow? "You're right," I added angrily. "It *is* toxic. Because of people like you."

I wanted to say more, but then Caitlin appeared, emerging from the girls' locker room with a big smile.

I brushed past Milo and ran over to give Caitlin a hug. "You were amazing," I told her, meaning it.

"Thanks," Caitlin said, hugging me back. "I can't believe I really got to play."

Milo walked over to us and tapped Caitlin on the shoulder. His face had relaxed into a proud smile, and the way he gazed at Caitlin made my stomach sink. *Wait.* Did Milo *like* Caitlin? When had that happened? Did Caitlin even realize it? Probably not. She was often oblivious about stuff like that.

"Hey, Stone," he told Caitlin. "Good game tonight. You made your first extra point. That's got to feel great."

"Thanks," Caitlin said to him cautiously. "You were great, too." She frowned, glancing from me to Milo. The tension was thick in the air.

"Thanks," Milo said, "but you made history."

"Yeah," I said, taking Caitlin's arm and pulling her away. "She did. Come on," I added to Caitlin, "we've got to go find Luna."

Then we hurried off, leaving Milo far behind us.

◌   ◌   ◌

"You know you can't trust him, right?" I said to Caitlin when she, Luna, and I were in my car, heading home.

"Milo?" Luna said from the back seat, glancing at me and Caitlin up front. I'd filled her and Caitlin in on my interaction with him as soon as we'd left the school.

I nodded. My eyes were on the road, but my hands gripped the steering wheel so tightly my knuckles felt like they would pop out of my skin.

"I know," said Caitlin. She rearranged her legs restlessly. "He's a jerk, of course. We've always known that." She paused.

"But?" I prompted.

Caitlin sighed. "He's my teammate now. I have to learn to live with him. I can hate him for what he did to you, but we still need to work together." She was quiet a minute, then added, "I know he has his faults. But we all do."

My stomach twisted and I didn't answer. It was true; my biggest fault at the moment was that I was lying to my friends about the vow. While Caitlin was so busy trying to fight her way onto the team, I was online betraying her trust. What kind of friend was I?

"Did he really say he wants to do the offline challenge?" Luna asked, leaning forward, as if she'd read my mind. "Having someone super popular like him join in could be huge." I knew she was thinking about her story.

"Yeah, he did, but I don't really believe he will," I said flatly.

When we got to my house, Luna jumped out of the car first. I turned to Caitlin beside me. She had grown quiet.

"Are you feeling okay?" I asked.

"Yeah, I'm just . . . tired," she said.

I nodded. "I don't want things to be weird between us because of Milo," I said.

She raked a hand through her hair and sighed. "Neither do I. Can we talk about something else? Something besides football? Or ChitChat?"

"Of course," I said. *Anything but ChitChat.* Then I had an idea. "Let's do something just the two of us, from the offline list." I snapped my fingers. "I know. Take a lesson."

Caitlin squinted at me. I reached over her and opened the glove compartment to take out a flyer that someone had placed under my windshield wiper last week. "Look."

Caitlin glanced down at the flyer. The black block letters read SALSA DANCING, BLUE AGAVE ROOM, TUESDAY. LESSONS START AT 7:00.

"Seriously?" Caitlin said, raising her eyebrows at me.

"Hey, you didn't do the ghost tour," I told her. "You owe me one activity. Besides, I hear dancing is great for your coordination."

Caitlin laughed. "Fine, I'll do it."

I clapped my hands. "You won't regret it."

We got out of the car and joined Luna, who was waiting for us impatiently outside my front door.

"Cait, do you know which movie you want to watch tonight?" Luna asked.

Caitlin smirked at me. "Sure. How about *Dirty Dancing*?"

And that made me laugh, too.

CHAPTER TWENTY

A sister can be seen as someone who is both ourselves and very much not ourselves—a special kind of double.

—Toni Morrison

When I got to the shelter on Monday, Isco came with me into Rocco's kennel and showed me all the commands Rocco knew—*sit, down, come,* and *stay.* I was impressed.

"Did you teach him?" I asked.

"He came already knowing most," Isco said. "He's a smart dog, but it probably means he had a family once."

"What happened?" I asked, feeling a pang of sadness.

"Who knows?" Isco said, leaning down to scratch Rocco behind the ears. "All these animals have so many stories we'll never know. But he's here now—and you're here now—and that's what is important."

Rocco's tail thudded against the concrete floor. He knew we were talking about him.

Isco smiled. "He bonds deeply. It will be a good thing when he finds the right match."

"But he will find someone?" I asked.

"Someone will find him," Isco said. "You wait and see."

I hoped he was right. I knelt down and rubbed Rocco's broad head. He watched me expectantly, and I gave him the little chew toy I'd bought for him the other day. He pounced on it eagerly.

"How old is Rocco?" I asked, watching him play with the toy.

"Don't know for sure," Isco said, "but we think he's around eight years old."

"How long do dogs live?" I asked.

"It's hard to say. A dog his size might live until he's ten or twelve."

"But that's not very long. Why would anyone adopt him when they know they might have to say goodbye to him so soon?" I tried not to cry, but the thought was so painful. There were too many goodbyes in my life.

"I guess that's why it's hard for older dogs to get adopted," Isco said quietly. "But you have to look at things the way Rocco does."

"What do you mean?" I asked, glancing up at Isco.

"Look at him. He's happy now. It's not about yesterday or tomorrow. It's about now," Isco said. "We could learn a lot from Rocco."

My eyes teared up, but I brushed them quickly away with the back of my hand before Isco could see. I looked over at Rocco and his chew toy.

"I forgot to bring something to read today," I realized out loud.

"Well, let's try something new," Isco suggested. "Teaching Rocco hand signals would be a great way to improve communication. He needs to understand the association between the verbal commands and the hand signals."

Rocco tilted his head to one side and looked at me like he agreed.

"Let's do it," I said.

"One finger pointing to the eye means watch me." Isco demonstrated. "Then you can show him an open hand, palm up, when you tell him to sit."

I tried it. Rocco learned quickly. "Should I give him a treat?" I asked.

"I think your praise is all he needs."

I rubbed Rocco's soft ears. "Good boy."

After Isco left us to practice, we tried the commands a few more times, and it was clear Rocco was picking up on all of them. I decided to take Rocco outside as a little reward.

"It's a beautiful day for a walk," I said, and Rocco's ears perked up.

The click of the leash onto his collar was like a lightning bolt. He leaned into my thigh, tail wagging. Somewhere in his past life, walks had been a very good thing.

I took him out past the front desk, and I waved to Isco. "Have fun!" he called to us, and Rocco's tail wagged.

While we walked around the block, Rocco glanced at the people passing by, but never tried to pull or leave my side. We crossed the street at the corner and passed a hair salon.

I looked down at Rocco. "Do you think I should cut

my hair?" I asked him. Getting the pink streak in my hair had been fun and freeing. Now I wanted something more. Sometimes the weight of my hair felt heavy, like a blanket full of boulders.

Rocco glanced up at me, and I was sure he was saying yes.

After the walk, Rocco lay by my side on the floor of his kennel and dreamed of running. His feet twitched in his sleep, and sometimes he made excited little yelps. I wondered if he dreamed of running in grassy meadows or swimming in lakes chasing a green tennis ball. I tried to calm him with soft strokes and mumbled words that everything was going to be okay, but then I just let him run.

It was getting harder to say goodbye, but eventually I knew I had to leave. I waved to Isco at the desk on my way out.

"Hey, Annie?" Isco said before I stepped out the door.

I glanced back at him, suddenly feeling a little nervous, although not in a bad way. "Um, yeah?" I asked.

I noticed Isco looked sort of nervous, too. He came around from behind the desk. "Would you, uh, want to do something sometime?"

I looked at him and blinked.

"With me," he clarified.

I felt my heart leap.

"Like what?" I asked.

"I have my break in a few minutes. We could grab a coffee at Mugs or something."

That sounded too much like a date, and I wasn't ready for anything like that.

But . . .

I looked at Isco. He was undeniably cute. And sweet. And probably more thoughtful than Jameson had ever been. But was I even over Jameson?

"I have to be home for dinner tonight. My sister is having her fiancé's family over." I talked really fast, and my voice sounded high pitched even to me. "Anyway, it's like a big deal."

"No problem," he said quickly.

Then I looked at him again. His eyes were so dark brown I almost couldn't see the black of his irises.

"But I could walk with you over to Mugs," I said. "It's on my way to where I parked."

It wasn't.

He smiled.

We walked slowly back to the square through Trimble Court Alley. The zigzag string of lights overhead lit up the brick walls and the hanging flower baskets. Up ahead was an outdoor piano, painted with exuberant red and green dots. Brightly painted pianos were placed all over town, a partnership with local artists and the city. Isco walked over to an upright piano and sat down on the bench.

"Do you play?" I asked, surprised. What else was I

going to learn about him? He patted the empty spot beside him, and I sat down on the bench.

Isco laid his hands lightly on the keys, then slowly began to play. The melody was beautiful, but I had never heard it before. I was mesmerized as I watched his fingers moving lightly over the keys. When he stopped, we let the silence linger.

"That was beautiful," I whispered. He looked over at me, and I felt butterflies in my stomach. Oh my God. Was he going to kiss me? No. It couldn't be. Quickly, I shoved his chest, laughing and shaking my head to break the spell. "I'm sure you serenade all the girls."

"Nope. I don't use my obvious musical talent to win over girls."

I rolled my eyes, still laughing, glad that the awkward moment had passed. "So what *do* you use?" I teased.

"Hmm." Isco pretended to think hard. "I have some great opening lines. You want to hear them?" he asked with a grin.

"Sure," I groaned.

"If you were a library book, I would check you out."

I groaned again. "That's terrible."

"I know," he said. "Wait. How about this one?" He straightened up on the bench, then made his face super serious. "Are you a camera? Because every time I look at you, I smile."

I burst out laughing. I couldn't believe he said it with a straight face. "These are going from bad to worse."

"Sorry," Isco said, his eyes sparkling. "You asked."

He looked directly at me again, and I stopped laughing. Why did he have to have such thick black hair that fell back down over one eye no matter how many times he brushed it away? His glance dropped down to my lips. Neither of us was laughing now. My pulse was pounding. Slamming.

I shouldn't like him. Even if I did. I shouldn't.

"Annie," Isco said quietly. "Would it be all right if I kissed you?"

He slowly leaned toward me, and for a moment I leaned toward him, but I pulled away. No more broken hearts for me. Even if it meant missing out on stomach flutters and amazing kisses. Even if it meant missing out on what felt like a real connection with Isco. I had to protect myself.

Isco's brow furrowed. I stood up suddenly from the piano bench.

"I'm sorry," I said. "I have to go."

⏻ ⏻ ⏻

When Savanna walked into my bedroom, she stopped in her tracks. I sat in front of my mirror, with my scissors in one hand and a big chunk of hair in the other. The bright pink streak in front was now only six inches long.

"Annie, what are you doing?" she gasped. "Miguel and his parents are gonna be here in an hour—"

"Jameson and I broke up," I blurted. Tears were running down my face continuously, but I wasn't making any noise. I wasn't sure whether I was crying about Jameson or the hair. Or everything.

"You did?" Savanna said, looking more shocked by that than by my haircut. "When?"

"A while ago," I said. "I didn't want to tell you because you were so busy with wedding stuff . . . and you wanted him to be an usher . . . and . . . and it happened over ChitChat, so that's why I haven't been going online, but I've been going back on now in secret, and . . . and . . ."

"Annie," Savanna said. "It's okay. You're going to be okay."

She walked over to me and wrapped her arms around me. That's when I started to sob, big, ugly, gulping sobs. Savanna stroked my back and let me cry.

"Jameson never wanted me to cut my hair," I said through my sobs. "He said it looked so pretty long. He didn't even like it when I got a trim." I caught my breath. "He didn't have the right to keep me from cutting it." I held out the chunk of hair, and Savanna took it out of my hand, not sure what to do with it. "It's *my* hair."

"It is," Savanna said with a nod. "Is that why you cut your hair?" she asked after a while. "Because of Jameson?"

I ran my hand through what was left of my hair, the tears slowing. "It seemed like a good idea at the time," I sniffed. Savanna smiled, and I cracked a smile, too. "It wasn't really because of Jameson. I actually think I'm over him." I scooched over so Savanna could sit beside me on the chair. "At first, when we broke up, all I could think about were the happy memories. But you know, not everything with him was so great."

"I knew that," Savanna said wisely. "I wouldn't have said anything, because you seemed happy. But I didn't think you guys would be together forever."

I shrugged. "I just wish things didn't have to change. Everything is changing."

Savanna nodded. "I know this may sound corny," she said, "but sometimes things *have* to change. And it hurts. But it's not always bad in the end. Like, I'm excited to get married and start a new life with Miguel, but I'm sad it won't be the same here at home. A big part of my life had to change for something wonderful to begin."

"But you're leaving me," I said with a big sob. *There. I finally said it.* I wasn't happy about the wedding.

Savanna blinked. "I'll never leave you, Annie. No matter where I am, I'll always be your sister. That's never going to change."

Something inside me loosened just a bit. For the first time, I felt a surge of happiness for Savanna. She deserved her happy ever after, and I was selfish to think of only what I was losing.

"How does my hair look?" I asked, wiping at my eyes with the sleeve of my sweater.

"Well . . ." Savanna waited a few breaths before she answered. Now was not the time to lie. "It's just hair. It will grow back."

That was not a good sign.

"Besides, pixie cuts are really in style?" Savanna offered with a shrug.

I laughed. And then Savanna laughed.

"Let me see what I can do," Savanna said, getting to her feet and reaching for the scissors. "I've been known to fix a hair disaster or two in my day."

"Thanks," I said as Savanna stood behind me to examine my hair. I wiped the remaining tears off my face and smiled at my sister in the mirror.

CHAPTER TWENTY-ONE

Every day brings a chance for you to draw in a breath, kick off
your shoes, and dance.

—Oprah Winfrey

"Your hair!" Caitlin exclaimed when we met on the sidewalk outside the Rio. Her mouth dropped open.

"Do you like it?" I asked self-consciously, patting the
back of my head. Luckily, Savanna had worked wonders
on my chop job, and now I thought I might even like the
new me. At least my hair.

"I love it," Caitlin said, admiring the hairdo from all
sides. "It looks so chic."

"Thanks," I said, grinning. For a moment, I imagined
posting a selfie of my new hair to ChitChat and what the
comments would be. But then I pushed the thought away.
It was bad enough I'd gone back on ChitChat last night
after the dinner with Miguel and his parents.

I nodded toward the unmarked door beside the restaurant and asked, "You ready for this?" Caitlin and I could
both hear the music coming from the second floor.

"As ready as I'm going to get." Caitlin opened the door
to reveal steep steps leading upstairs. "After you," she
said, and followed me up the steps toward the pounding
beat above our heads.

The top of the stairs opened into a large room with hardwood floors and arching windows overlooking the street below. It was a huge dance studio with a DJ set up in one corner. A few folding chairs lined the exposed brick walls, but no one was sitting in them. Instead, couples and small groups of people milled around, chatting. Caitlin immediately headed for a chair and safety.

Caitlin was not exactly the most graceful person on a dance floor. Not even close. It was surprising considering her athleticism. People naturally assumed she would be just as agile and fluid when following a beat as she was on the soccer or football field. After years of birthday-party DJs and school dances, I knew she was not. Maybe that's why, when I picked salsa dancing as our activity, she hadn't been thrilled. But I was determined. It's not like I was a great dancer either—I mostly felt like a klutz at every school dance I'd ever gone to. And now I was going to embarrass myself in front of a whole new group of strangers. But maybe tonight I'd be so tired from dancing, I wouldn't want to go online.

"I'll just watch first," Caitlin told me. "Good luck."

"No way," I said. "You need to experience this firsthand."

A handsome man wearing a yellow shirt and jeans walked into the center of the room. He clapped his hands together three times.

"Welcome, everyone," he said.

I grabbed Caitlin's hand and pulled her out toward the dance floor.

"Circle up," the man said. "My name is Javier and I'll be your dance instructor for the night."

Caitlin and I were by far the youngest in the room. We found ourselves standing beside a short gray-haired man. I smiled lamely toward the man, already feeling sorry that he'd have to see me dance. He beamed back, leaning in to introduce himself. "My name is Clyde and this is my wife, Tinka."

The tiny gray-haired woman beside Clyde enthusiastically shook my hand.

"I'm Annie," I said. "And this is my friend Caitlin."

"Such pretty young ladies," Tinka said with a smile. "I can tell you're going to be naturals at this."

Caitlin and I exchanged a glance. *Glad somebody thinks so.*

Javier managed to get everyone's attention and started with the basic step. "Rock your body weight forward," he called out. "Swing your hips as you shift your body weight. March your feet in rhythm to the beat of the music. One, two, three. Pause. One, two, three. Pause."

Everyone practiced. I tried to move rhythmically to the beat and follow along, keeping my eyes fixed on Javier instead of my own feet. But no matter how hard I tried, it felt like I was just a second too late. I glanced at Caitlin. I could tell this was way outside her comfort zone, but her steps were surer than mine. She wasn't totally embarrassing herself.

I looked over at Clyde. It was a mistake. Clyde was an amazing dancer, smoothly moving through the steps. It was obvious he'd done this before. Tinka didn't seem to be having much trouble either.

But I wasn't ready to admit defeat.

Javier glided back and forth, back and forth in the middle of the circle. He was impossibly smooth and effortless. "Now we will try it with a partner. Everyone?"

Caitlin turned to bow before me. "Would you like to dance?" she asked.

"Of course," I said.

I felt incredibly awkward at first—out of step, just off the beat. It didn't help that Caitlin was starting to giggle. My brows knitted together in concentration, and my lips moved as I counted the steps. I would have been laughing, too, if I wasn't working so hard at keeping up. My breathing quickened, and I looked up from watching my feet to see Caitlin's huge grin. I felt myself relax. We were having fun. Together.

The music was contagious—lively and upbeat with lots of percussion—and the crowd forgiving. I quickly realized I needed to stop being so hard on myself. All around us, couples were moving and smiling. People made mistakes. And it was okay. Completely swept up in the music, my breathing got faster and my smile wider. The room pulsed around me. I forgot about counting and my feet moving just the right way. Instead, it was all about letting the music help me along.

Suddenly, I felt like my friends and I should have always gone out dancing every day. I thought of all the hours I'd spent on ChitChat instead of doing other things. It was like I'd been away somewhere and missed out on everything.

Dancing took more energy than expected, and when the third song ended, I was completely out of breath. "I need a break," I told Caitlin, and we headed toward the folding chairs along the wall.

"How'd I do?" Caitlin asked.

"Fishing for a compliment?"

"Would it kill you?"

"You're pretty good at this," I said finally. "Better than I expected."

"YouTube," she admitted, with a slight grin.

I laughed. "That's cheating."

She raised her hands in protest. "We didn't make any rules about watching videos!"

"Okay, but I still think you had the advantage," I said.

"It was definitely easier with an actual partner." Caitlin nudged me and I laughed again.

We sat and watched Tinka and Clyde move seamlessly in perfect synchrony. It was impossible not to smile. For a moment, my hand itched to pull out a phone and record a video: #smooth #beat #happy. I looked over at Caitlin. She felt it, too.

"I'm jealous," she said.

I pulled my hair up off my sweaty neck with one hand, fanning my face with the other. "Because they're such good dancers and we never will be?"

"No, silly." Caitlin fake-punched my arm, then tried to articulate her thoughts. "It's because they have each other." She started, then stopped. She tried again. "My dad is a really good dancer."

"Seriously?" I was surprised. Coach Stone did not seem like the dancing type.

"I know. You wouldn't think at his size, he'd be that graceful, but you should see him dance at wedding receptions and family events. I loved to watch him and my mom . . ." Her voice trailed off, and she swallowed hard, letting the music fill up the beat of silence between us. She rubbed the back of her hand against her forehead.

"They were good together," she finally said with a shrug.

I studied her profile while Caitlin watched the dancers. She looked so young, with flushed cheeks and tendrils of brown hair around her face. In that moment, I thought Cait looked a lot like her mother. I didn't know whether to tell her or not, if it would make her sad or happy.

"Can I have this dance?" I asked instead. I stood up and held out my hand. She took it without hesitation.

⟳ ⟳ ⟳

Later we hung out in my bedroom devouring the pepperoni pizza we picked up on the way home. Evidently dancing made us ravenous. We'd texted Luna to see if she wanted to join us, but she was hard at work on her story.

"I have a new idea for the list," Caitlin said suddenly.

I swallowed my bite of pizza, then said, "I think we've already done plenty for tonight."

She waved half a piece of pizza toward me. "No, seriously. This one is easy."

I eyed her suspiciously. "What?"

"Build a fort," she said. "Remember how we used to do that right here in your room?"

That actually sounded good. Comforting. Relaxing.

It took a few minutes to remember how to drape the blankets from the bed to the desk chair, but eventually we constructed a huge tentlike structure that took up most of the room. Satisfied, we reclined on pillows inside and grinned conspiratorially at each other. I crawled out to retrieve the pizza box, then pulled it back inside.

"We should tell secrets," Caitlin said.

My mind immediately jumped to the vow. "Why?"

"That's what you do inside forts. It's like a rule."

"Are you sure?" *Not big secrets.*

Caitlin nodded enthusiastically.

"You go first," Caitlin said, and I desperately tried to think of some other secret besides admitting how I was still going back on ChitChat.

"I think I like dogs. Or maybe just one dog."

"Why is that a secret?" Caitlin asked.

"Because I've never told anyone about it."

"It's not a very big secret," Caitlin said.

I smiled. "Okay, maybe it's more than just liking a dog. I think I like a boy, too."

Caitlin looked confused. "Where is all this happening?"

"I started volunteering at the animal shelter, and I met this dog, Rocco, there. He's amazing."

Caitlin narrowed her eyes at me. "Get to the part about the boy."

"Isco works at the shelter and we've been talking . . ." My voice trailed off.

Caitlin snapped her fingers. "I *knew* there was something strange about him popping up everywhere."

"I think he's nice. And funny. And . . ."

"And?"

My heart thumped. I closed my eyes and put my head down on my crossed arms. "We almost kissed."

There. I said it. There was silence. I lifted my head and looked at Caitlin.

"Wow." Caitlin blinked, then grinned. "That *is* a big secret."

"Now you," I said.

Caitlin said it as quick as possible. Like ripping off a Band-Aid. "I think I like Milo."

I sat up straight. "You *what*?"

Caitlin tried to explain. "I didn't plan it."

I crawled out of the fort, and Caitlin followed slowly. The fun was over. She'd ruined it. I sat on my bed, jaw clenched.

"I'm sorry. Please, Annie, listen," Caitlin pleaded. "I know I should have told you sooner. It just—just kind of happened over the past few days."

"So now you've told me. You don't have to sneak around anymore."

"We haven't even gone out or anything! But I like him and I think he likes me, too." She sat down beside me. "He's been really supportive of my being on the team. Which has been a surprise."

I balled my hands into fists. "Have you told Luna?"

Beside me, Caitlin nodded, and I felt a stab of pain.

"I know you don't like him," Caitlin said.

"Of course I don't," I snapped. "He ruined my life."

Caitlin looked down. "I mean, yeah, the video sucked. But Milo really feels terrible about posting it now. He asked me what he can do to make it up to you."

"He can leave me alone," I said icily. I stared at Caitlin, then turned around to face the wall. "And so can you."

"Seriously?" Caitlin said.

I didn't answer. I felt her stand up but didn't turn to look.

"Okay, I'm gonna go now," Caitlin said, waiting for a beat. I didn't move. She headed for the door, but I stayed put—back rigid and unyielding, even as tears filled my eyes.

And even worse than our fight? I knew that once Caitlin was gone, nothing would stop me from going back on ChitChat.

Facts

★ 500 million tweets sent every day
★ 70 million images uploaded on ChitChat every day
★ 2 billion worldwide social network users
★ 300 hours of video uploaded per minute on YouTube
★ Average person checks their phone 150 times a day.

95% of teens have access to a smartphone, and 45% say they are online "almost constantly."

On any given day, teens in the United States spend about nine hours using social media.

Nine hours.

That's more time than we spend sleeping, eating, or going to school.

Links between social media and anxiety and depression??? Check facts . . .

Social media is the biggest game teenagers engage in on a daily basis.

That's it—my headline.

Luna

CHAPTER TWENTY-TWO

*The most common way people give up their power is by thinking
they don't have any.*

—Alice Walker

I sat on the stool at the coffee bar beside Luna, waiting
to lie.

Her laptop was open, and her hands poised over the
keyboard. We were about to start our interview for her
story, and I could feel how excited Luna was.

#OfflineOctober seemed to only be growing. The list
of signatures had more students committed to the vow
than we'd ever dreamed. In the cafeteria, you could see
the change—people talked to each other and didn't stare
at their phones. People were participating in the offline
activities, going on hikes and reading more books. And it
was all thanks to Luna, really.

"Are you ready?" Luna asked me.

A cliff face of fear loomed in front of me. It was one
thing to be dishonest with your closest friends, but now,
in the article, I'd be going public. I waited for the first
question, a hollow smile plastered to my face.

"How has being offline changed you?"

Think. Think. Think, I chanted inside my brain.

"I just notice things more," I finally said. "I'm more

in the moment. It feels like I'm experiencing things for myself, not just watching other people do things." Which, I realized, was true. In the times when I was able to step away from my phone, I *did* feel that way. So maybe I wasn't lying quite so much.

Luna typed quickly and smiled at the screen.

"If you wanted to give someone younger advice about social media before they started using it, what would you say?" she asked.

"People post their best moments online, so don't compare your life to what you see. Real life isn't going to be as perfect as all the posed shots you see on social media." As I spoke, I wished I could really and truly follow my own advice.

Luna nodded solemnly. "Great advice."

"Just ask yourself, did that ChitChat scroll make you feel better or worse?" I added, as if I were some expert.

"Perfect. Can I quote you on that?" Luna asked, typing hard.

I nodded, feeling like a fraud.

I looked down at my cup. If I could access ChitChat now, I would take a picture of the perfect foam heart on top of the cappuccino. It looked so delicious in the bright yellow cup set against the green-tiled counter. I even knew what to tag it on the post. #cappuccinoart #baristagram #lifeisgood #cupofperfection

Luna wrinkled her brow. "What's wrong?"

I slumped on the stool, rubbing my palms against my forehead. "Nothing. I had a fight with Caitlin."

"I heard."

I stared at her. "And you think this thing with Milo is okay?"

"I didn't say that," Luna said, holding up her hands in surrender. "I don't want to get caught in the middle."

I picked up the coffee cup, then set it back down without taking a sip. My fear peaked and then leveled out. My heart rate slowed. Now was the time to come clean and tell Luna I wasn't being honest about the vow. I took a deep breath.

"Luna," I began, "I have something I want to—"

The door to the coffee shop opened, and the two freshman fashionistas, Kiyana and Lizzie, arrived with a burst of cold air. Kiyana wore a cherry-red turtleneck with a denim miniskirt, her curly brown hair clipped back with silver barrettes. Lizzie had a completely different look, with a slate-blue slip dress and a long, cozy cardigan. I wondered if they felt their efforts were completely in vain without ChitChat to capture the looks.

"Hi!" Luna called, waving them over. "I'm almost done interviewing Annie."

"What are they doing here?" I whispered to her as the two girls approached.

"They volunteered to help with some ideas for the Fall Festival," Luna said, her eyes bright. "Remember how we're planning to give certificates to the #OfflineOctober participants?"

Oh right. My stomach sank. I'd forgotten about that. And hadn't Luna wanted me and Caitlin to make some sort of speech onstage? This was getting more and more complicated.

Lizzie and Kiyana sat down at the coffee bar, grinning at me and Luna.

"Go, Team SO." Lizzie shook her fists in the air like she was shaking pom-poms.

"We took a hike this morning," Kiyana announced triumphantly. "No phones!"

"That's awesome, guys," Luna said, giving both the girls high fives. I just smiled weakly.

Luna turned back to me. "Annie, you were about to say something? For the article?" She raised her eyebrows at me, her fingers back on her laptop keyboard, ready to type.

I swallowed hard. I'd been ready to confess to Luna that I hadn't been keeping the vow. But I couldn't tell her now, not in front of Lizzie and Kiyana, who were so sweet and eager about #OfflineOctober.

"No, it was nothing," I said quickly. "Nothing important."

"Okay," Luna said, frowning at me. She could tell something was up, but I hoped she'd just drop it. "I think I have enough quotes from you for the article for now. We can always pick it up again later."

"Sure," I said dully.

"Now," Luna said, turning back to Lizzie and Kiyana. "I'm glad you guys are here. I have some big news about the Fall Festival."

"What?" I asked, suddenly worried.

Luna beamed. "I told Tamar that we were planning some sort of ceremony for #OfflineOctober at the Fall Festival, and word got around, and now apparently a Denver news station is interested in the story!"

I gasped, and so did Lizzie and Kiyana. This was bigger than I'd even imagined.

"What does that mean?" I asked nervously.

"They might send a reporter to the Festival," Luna explained, her voice high with excitement. "Apparently they think it's a timely story, this idea of going offline."

"Omg," Lizzie said. "Whatever we do at the Festival for the participants has to be huge now."

Everyone nodded enthusiastically.

Except me.

Luna tapped a finger on the side of her cheek, eyes narrowed, thinking. "Instead of certificates . . . what about awards?" she said.

My stomach lurched at the thought of walking across the stage to accept an award I didn't earn.

There was a long pause while the three of them thought.

"Maybe people get more recognition the *longer* they've been offline," Kiyana said. She gestured to me and Luna. "After all, you've been offline for a month."

I've only been offline for twenty-four hours. No one needed to know that, though. I nodded.

"That's a great idea," Luna said enthusiastically. "Let me discuss that with Ms. Spencer and the student council team, and see what we can do."

I shifted on my stool. Maybe the idea wouldn't work. It sounded sort of convoluted anyway. Would people on Team SO just share how long they'd been offline? I supposed I could keep lying then.

But it felt so wrong.

I heard Luna's phone buzz in her pocket.

"Sorry," she said, taking it out. "This might be my mom or dad." When she looked at the screen, though, her eyes got huge and a grin spread across her face.

"What is it?" I asked, scared that it was something more about #OfflineOctober or the Denver news station.

"Caitlin just texted me," Luna said. "Eli Vernon has the flu. He can't play in the game Friday!" Luna looked up at me with a big smile. "Our girl is going to play for real in the championship game."

Wow. I was torn between feeling proud and excited for Caitlin, and also sad that she hadn't texted me the news, too. I hadn't heard my phone buzz. I pulled it out just to double-check. No new messages. Luna saw my face fall, and she reached out to squeeze my arm. She understood.

This was the longest Caitlin and I had ever gone without talking. Last night, I stood at my window looking across the way to her house for some sign, but her curtains stayed closed. I refused to accept that our friendship was over, though. A boy had never come between us before, and it wasn't going to happen now. Even if I had to accept that boy might be Milo. I could only hope I'd get a chance to talk to Caitlin either before the game, or afterward, at the Fall Festival.

"That's so awesome," Kiyana was saying. "If Caitlin helps the team win, she's almost guaranteed a starting spot on the team next year."

Lizzie, Kiyana, and Luna all began chatting excitedly about the game and Caitlin.

I was quiet, looking down at my phone.

Caitlin was playing in the big game. Her dream was coming true.

Jameson's dream was happening, too. Discord was headlining the Fall Festival.

Luna was about to write the biggest story of her life, which could mean her dream of being editor in chief would come true.

And what about me? What did my destiny hold? I had no idea. But I did know one thing. I was going to stop going on ChitChat. For real. No more cheating. I had to at least stick it out until the Fall Festival. I couldn't keep lying to my friends, to the rest of Team SO, to everyone.

Dear Chitchat,

I'm a liar. I told everyone I left you, But I didn't. You're still in my life even bigger than before. I don't want you here. Not on your terms. We're not good for each other. You control the shots. You control me.

But we're done. For real. For now.

Annie

○ ○ ○

I did it. I finished the article about the offline vow, and I emailed it to Tamar. I barely slept, but I think it was worth it.

Now I just have to wait for her to read it. I hope she thinks it's good. I hope she thinks it says something true.

But no matter what happens, I'll be proud of what I wrote.

Luna

○ ○ ○

On the night of the big game, I will be in the girls' locker room getting ready. No one will document this part. There will be only me.

There is a whole ritual. First, I unwrap the big square of sugary bubble gum, put it in my mouth, and start to chew. While it is loosening up to just the right popping consistency, I'll start putting on my shoulder pads. Then the jersey over the top. It's hot and heavy, but I try to think of it like a gladiator shield. It is exactly what's needed before going into battle.

There is even a smell. It is sort of a mixture of bubble gum, leather, and dirt.

Most people never know what it feels like to be the best, but I'm not like most people. This is what I was meant to do.

Cait

CHAPTER TWENTY-THREE

A ship is safe in harbor, but that's not what ships are for.

—John A. Shedd

On the night of the big game and the Fall Festival, I'd been offline for two days. It felt good. I felt strong. I could do this.

Luna and I sat together in the packed stands along with everyone else in the school, watching the game—and Caitlin.

Caitlin was amazing out there—she had a great kickoff and a couple of awesome punts. But there hadn't yet been an opportunity for her to help put points on the board.

Mariah was sitting in front of us, wearing a tunic-length forest-green hoodie over black leggings tucked into tall buckled boots. She looked like she could have been a cover model in a fall fashion shoot. She gave me a quick look over one shoulder, and I smiled at her, relishing the way she jerked her head back around to look straight ahead.

In the stands, each school's fans cheered whenever their team moved the ball up the field, and groaned whenever the opposing team did the same. The game was scoreless until Rocky Mountain scored a touchdown with only five minutes left on the clock. Then they missed the kick for the extra point after, leaving a tiny window of hope for us.

When Davis threw the ball way downfield to Milo with only a minute left on the clock, both sides of the stands held their breath. The ball hung suspended for what seemed like an eternity, and then Milo leaped into the air above the end zone.

Touchdown!

The crowd went wild. Luna and I celebrated, screaming and jumping up and down. The noise was deafening. Now was the moment Caitlin had trained and waited for. The game was tied 6-6. One kick to send the ball between the goalposts and Fort Collins would win the championship.

It was all up to her. I could hear echoes of the cheering for Milo's touchdown, but now all I could feel was my heart pounding away inside me.

Caitlin's dad stepped out in front of her, smiling and holding out a glove-covered fist. If he was nervous for her, he didn't show it. Caitlin bumped her own fist against his. She nodded at him, but kept looking straight ahead toward the field. I knew the kick had already started in her mind. It was like walking out onstage for a huge performance. She pulled her helmet on and jogged out to huddle with the guys. She was ready. The crowd was ready, too. There was an excited murmur in the completely full stands.

Her stage. Her magic.

"You got this," I whispered, even though I knew she couldn't hear me. But I hoped she could feel me—and Luna—out here, rooting for her.

"We've saved the best until last." The announcement

echoed back up the mountain. "This is what we've all been waiting for . . . Caitlin Stone comes in for the extra point."

The sound of the crowd got even louder.

Caitlin took three steps back, and the ball was snapped to the holder. Everything was moving so fast. The guys on the other team ran directly toward Caitlin as fast as they could. Caitlin ran toward the ball. Her foot connected to the ball, and it soared toward the goalposts. I watched the ball, just like everyone else in the stadium.

I held my breath.

The ball went through the goalposts.

She did it.

The stands erupted again as time ran out on the clock. It was over. We were the district champions, and it was all due to Caitlin. Luna and I screamed and jumped up and down along with the rest of the crowd.

"Oh no." Luna stopped jumping, her face suddenly ashen. She pointed toward the field. Caitlin was sitting still on the grass, holding her ankle. Milo was kneeling on the ground beside her, the rest of the team hovering behind his shoulder. My heart dropped. Something was wrong.

Caitlin's dad ran out onto the field. He looked terrified as he crouched down next to Caitlin, talking softly to her. I grabbed Luna's hand. The stands stood in hushed silence, watching and waiting. Cait looked so small and so far away.

"Stand up," I breathed.

Caitlin's dad suddenly got to his feet and then held his hand down toward her. She took it and got to her feet, slowly. Her dad hugged her, and the crowd erupted joy-fully again. Caitlin lifted her arm in salute and then was instantly engulfed by her celebrating teammates.

"She's okay," I said breathlessly.

"She's a lot more than okay. She's amazing," Luna said.

"We have to go," I said, pushing past the people stand-ing beside us. I had to congratulate Caitlin in person. But mostly I wanted to tell her how sorry I was about everything.

○ ○ ○

We found Caitlin outside the stadium gates. Her dad stood on one side of her, Milo on the other. It was like a fortress. I tried to catch her eye, but it wasn't easy with the crowd around her.

Luna pushed her way through the people, and I followed a step behind. Luna cupped her hands over her mouth and yelled toward a beaming Caitlin, "Congratulations!"

Caitlin shoved Iain and Milo out of the way and stepped into Luna's wide-open arms and tight hug. She caught my eye over Luna's shoulder.

"I'm sorry," I whispered, not looking away.

Caitlin untangled herself from Luna and stepped toward me.

"Are you okay?" I asked, looking her up and down for any sign of injury.

"Yeah. Just a little shaken up on the play. I'm fine."

The noisy crowd pulsed around us, still celebrating. I

leaned in to talk directly into Caitlin's ear. "I was wrong to get upset with you."

When I pulled away, she was smiling. She put her arm around me. "It just proves we shouldn't keep secrets from each other. You'd think we would have learned that by now, right?"

My stomach churned. I needed to come clean about the vow. But the crowd jostled at our elbows and Cait was getting pulled away.

Luna called out, "We'll see you at the Fall Festival?"

Caitlin smiled and yelled back over her shoulder, "I wouldn't miss it."

Right. The Fall Festival. Somehow in all the excitement and drama of the game, I'd forgotten about it.

"You and Caitlin have to accept your Offline Awards," Luna said, putting her arm around my shoulder. "You've earned it."

I didn't earn anything.

"I actually need to head over there now to set things up with Ms. Spencer," Luna was saying. She gave me a quick hug. "I'll see you at the Festival?"

I nodded and watched her run off toward her car. I knew I had to keep pretending, at least for tonight. I would go onstage for Luna, for the moment she'd planned. And then I could return to my ChitChat prison later.

CHAPTER TWENTY-FOUR

Every lie is two lies—the lie we tell others and the lie we tell
ourselves to justify it.

—Robert Brault

Moth-filled floodlights lit up the crisp night, highlighting the two scarecrows perched on stacks of hay marking the entrance to the Fall Festival. I cupped my hands over my mouth to blow some warmth onto my frozen fingers. I wore a cozy oversized V-neck sweater, jeans, and white mesh sneakers. Some people were more dressed up, and I wondered while watching the crowd stream by if I should have tried harder with my outfit.

The band starting playing the fight song, and I pushed my uncertainties away. I headed in through the hand-painted cardboard arch. Smiling parent chaperones manned tables covered with hot dog fixings, chips, and drinks. Student council members, cheeks painted with sparkly pumpkins, handed out bright red-green-and-gold beaded necklaces to the incoming students, and I accepted one and looped it over my head. Excited yelps and screams came from the corn maze. Couples emerged clutching each other and giggling at their successful exit. I scanned the crowd for Luna, but she was nowhere in sight.

I had to admit the student council had done an amazing

job of carrying through on the theme. Nothing screamed fall more than pumpkins, hay, and a marching band. The buzz in the air was almost as strong as the smell of smoke from the strategically placed bonfires set up across the field. My hands itched to pull out my phone and take a picture to share, but I resisted.

Adam Chu was the DJ—he had one ear to a set of headphones, busy queuing up songs on his powerful-looking outdoor speakers. Behind him was the apple-bobbing booth, but there wasn't a line for that particular booth; my guess was that none of the girls wanted to mess up their carefully applied makeup dunking their face into a tub of water. Besides, it was cold enough without having a wet head. Maybe the plan for that booth had needed an editor's touch.

Jameson stepped out from behind a bale of hay.

"Hey," he said, looking right at me for the first time since we'd broken up. His eyes were the same golden-brown color. His hair still blond and curly. So why did he suddenly look like a stranger?

"Hi," I said as casually as I could while waiting for my heart to plummet. Strangely, it didn't. I didn't feel much of anything at all, except surprise at seeing him. "What's up?"

Jameson shrugged and shoved his hands into his pockets. "I like your hair."

"That's what you want to talk about?" I asked incredulously.

He laughed nervously. "No, but I do like it. You look adorable."

Once, not very long ago, I would have loved hearing him compliment my hair. Or my face. Or my outfit. Now I felt nothing except a faint buzz of confusion.

"Well, thanks," I said, thinking it was funny that he'd never wanted me to have shorter hair. "Are you nervous about your big debut?" I nodded toward the waiting instruments onstage.

He shrugged. "A little."

"I'm sure you'll do great." I glanced past him and saw Isco over by the stage talking with some friends of his. I hadn't seen Isco since that day he'd almost kissed me. I realized I missed hanging out with him and Rocco.

"I never said thank you."

I looked back at Jameson. "For what?"

"For always believing in Discord. For helping me get this gig."

I didn't know what to say.

"I can't stop thinking about you," Jameson said.

His words should have made me feel great. I'd imagined him saying something like this so many times. But instead I just felt irritated.

"I missed you, too," I finally said, but it came out like the missing part was over. And maybe it was. It finally, finally was.

"I made a huge mistake." Jameson watched me with

red-edged eyes. "We never should have broken up." He turned his face away, almost as though he was embarrassed to say it.

We *didn't break up,* I thought, but I didn't say anything.

"I want us to get back together," he said.

It should have been a question, but it wasn't. There was no asking about what *I* wanted. He stared at me, waiting for a response. I didn't feel hurried to give one. He noticed, and it made him uncomfortable. Then he did what he usually did when he ran out of things to talk to me about—he leaned forward and kissed me. The feel of his lips was familiar—warm and soft. But I didn't feel anything. And I didn't kiss him back. My lips were stiff and unmoving.

Surprised at the reception, he pulled back awkwardly. I watched him shifting his weight back and forth from one foot to another, all his bravado suddenly gone.

I waited for more, but he was waiting, too.

Finally I broke the silence between us. "Why did you even ask me out in the first place, Jameson?"

"Because I thought—still think—you're smart and beautiful and kind and . . . so many things."

"But you don't *like* me."

He frowned, confused. "Of course I *like* you."

"I don't think so," I said.

He blinked like he didn't hear me correctly. "You seem different."

"Look, nothing stays the same," I said, remembering

what Savanna had said. "Even if we want it more than anything."

He blinked again. "So you're saying you don't want to get back together?"

"I wanted to. So bad."

He ignored the past tense. "Me too."

"But I can't change who I am. Not even for you."

There was a tiny pause while Jameson processed my words. This wasn't going according to how he'd planned.

"I'm sorry," I said, but realized I wasn't and shouldn't have said it. "I've moved on."

Jameson thought that over. I watched him gather up the energy to keep trying. "Maybe we could just hang out sometimes?"

"I can't be your friend. Not yet," I said firmly.

I heard Jameson let a breath out, almost like a whimper. "But maybe someday?"

I nodded. "Maybe."

I stepped in and leaned my forehead against his shoulder. He slipped his arm around me. It felt so familiar, yet so different. Tears slipped down my cheeks.

He took the smallest of steps away from me. "So I'll see you around?"

I nodded, then said, "Wait." He turned to look back at me, his eyebrows raised hopefully.

Pausing for a minute, I was determined to keep my voice steady. "No matter what happens, I want you to be happy."

"I know," he said. "And I want the same for you."

Then he walked away, and I felt sad in a million different ways but also relieved. I sat on one of the hay bales that surrounded the fire, thinking about what just happened. I shifted uncomfortably, the hay pricking at my jeans. I looked over toward Isco again, but he was still talking to his friends. He hadn't seen Jameson kiss me. I wondered if I would tell him about it, if we spoke again.

"Can I talk to you?" Milo stood just outside the circle of hay bales, the fire flickering on his face.

I wanted to say no but shrugged instead. This apparently was the night for big conversations. "Do what you want."

I scooted over on the bale of hay, and he took a seat beside me, one knee bouncing up and down nervously. I didn't budge.

"What, Milo?" I finally asked.

"You want a hot dog?" He was stalling. We both knew it.

I nodded, although I really didn't, but it would give me a second to process all that was happening. Milo jumped up like a spark from the fire had lit his jeans and disappeared into the dark. While he was gone, I tried to compose myself. I wasn't going to give him the satisfaction of looking rattled. When he came back, he had two hot dogs already stuck on a long wire and two paper plates with buns. He perched on the bale beside me, then carefully handed one of the wires over. I resisted the urge to pull away, stubbornly claiming my space. I positioned the hot dog over the fire, trying to keep it from getting too close and immediately burning.

"Are you filming this?" I asked casually. "Going to post it to ChitChat later and see how many views you get?"

"No."

I looked carefully at him, but there was no sign of his usual cockiness. I swallowed hard and looked straight ahead toward the fire again.

"I wanted to say I was sorry for posting that video."

I didn't make eye contact. "I don't have to accept your apology."

"I know, but I had to say it."

I pulled in the hot dog to take a look. So far, so good. I moved to put it back into the fire and brushed against Milo's arm. I jerked back, and the hot dog almost fell off into the dirt.

He looked hurt at my obvious repulsion. "I don't have an excuse. It was a stupid thing to do and I did it without thinking; then I couldn't take it back."

My hot dog was starting to sizzle. I turned it slowly, thinking about how I'd broken the offline vow. Was Milo so much worse than me? I stared into the fire and remembered promises made.

As this fire is my witness, I vow to always stay friends.

No matter what.

No matter how.

I glanced over at him. "People screw up. It's what we do. All of us."

"He never said anything bad about you." We both knew who Milo was talking about. Jameson. We sat for a moment in silence. I took my hot dog off the fire and slid it into the waiting bun, but I didn't eat it.

Milo pulled his blackened hot dog out of the fire and surveyed it sadly. "Maybe I am the kind of person you think I am, but I don't want to be."

Both of us sat with our uneaten food on the plates in our laps, staring straight ahead. Evidently neither one of us was hungry. I could tell something else was bothering Milo, too.

"Caitlin's going to be okay," I said finally. "She wasn't hurt in the game."

"Am I that obvious?"

I laughed. It surprised us both. "Absolutely."

"She won't go out with me," Milo said.

I frowned. "Because of me?"

"No. Not entirely. But she is super loyal like that," he said. "She doesn't trust me. I don't blame her, after what I did."

"Maybe she's more forgiving than you think. And she doesn't have to choose between us," I said. "You should talk to her."

"Are you sure?"

I nodded. "But let me ask you one thing. Why do you like her?"

He looked surprised at the question, but then thought about it for a moment. "She's strong and bold and . . . gorgeous." His voice trailed off, then stopped as heat flamed up his neck in a red streak of color.

"I agree with you," I said. "And I'll tell her you said that when I get a chance."

Milo glanced up at me, looking grateful and hopeful all at once.

Up on the stage, Cheri, the student council president, picked up a handheld microphone and called out, "Hey. Hey. Hey." The cheerleaders yelled and bounced up and down in front wearing matching school sweatshirts. People responded with hand waves and catcalls. The marching band started playing the fight song, and everyone joined in to sing.

"I have to go," Milo said, and I nodded. He stood up from the bale of hay and walked off toward the lights. A few steps away, he turned. "Thank you," he said. I nodded.

The fight song ended, and Cheri stepped up to the front of the stage, fluttering her hands for quiet. She put her mouth close to the microphone. "Hello?"

The noise reduced to a small rumble. I saw Jameson waiting off to one side, his guitar slung over his shoulder. He was raking his hair out of his eyes and chewing nervously on his bottom lip.

"Everyone help me welcome Discord to the stage!" Cheri yelled into the microphone, and Jameson strutted out to center stage, his bandmates following. Jameson started strumming his guitar, and I recognized the song right away. It was a cover of Van Morrison's "Brown Eyed Girl." Hearing it was bittersweet. The band had obviously been practicing, and the song was much better than the first time I heard it in Jameson's garage last summer. I remembered how he changed the lyrics for me and sang, "My blue-eyed girl." That day, he finished off with a lazy grin that made my insides mush. Tonight, I felt more detached.

The crowd loved the song—everyone was dancing and singing along with the chorus. I glanced around at the happy people. I realized I was actually glad for Jameson. But my nerves shot up when I thought about the fact that I'd be up there on that stage next.

CHAPTER TWENTY-FIVE

One doesn't recognize the really important moments in one's life until it's too late.

—Agatha Christie

"Are you ready for the award ceremony?" Luna suddenly appeared out of the dark. She didn't wait for my answer. "The Channel 9 news team is here. Can you believe it?"

She pointed toward a white van to the right of the stage and a woman in a suit talking to a guy with a big camera on his shoulder. "They're going to film the ceremony."

My heart sank. I had to stop this now and tell her the truth. I had not kept the vow to stay off social media for a month. I hadn't even come close.

"Luna . . ." I started, but then Kiyana and Lizzie were there, babbling excitedly about the reporter.

"Oh. My. God. This is your chance to catch the attention of *real* journalists," Lizzie said, looking at Luna with an awed expression.

"Well, you guys came up with the brilliant idea for how to pick the award winners," Luna replied.

"How?" I asked worriedly.

"Ms. Spencer looked up all the names of the people who took the vow," Kiyana explained, "and checked all the names against their ChitChat accounts."

"Then she put the names and how long each person has been able to stay off ChitChat in these envelopes," Lizzie continued, and waved a handful of pale pink squares at me.

"How does she know?" I asked, my body growing cold.

"The ChitChat app records activity. It's in every profile; you just have to know where to look," Kiyana said proudly.

"Isn't that perfect?" Luna asked. "I didn't even think about that."

I didn't either.

"As I call out each name and the number of days they've been off ChitChat," Luna went on, "each person will come across the stage and get their award. You and Caitlin have the most days, of course, so you'll be last." She beamed proudly at me. "Cue biggest applause and the Channel 9 news team gets the whole thing on camera."

I reached for Luna's arm, but she was already gone, walking toward the stage with the girls. The comments were starting to scroll through my head again, louder than ever. My prison was telling me that I was an awful person, and it was right.

WHAT A JOKE! #LIAR

LIE MUCH???

DID I JUST SEE THAT GIRL STAB HER BESTIES IN THE BACK? 😊

Ms. Spencer stepped to center stage. She looked different with her dark curly hair down from her usual bun.

"Welcome, everyone!" she called out, waving to the crowd. "I'm delighted that one of our biggest stories this year is attracting some major media interest. It is an important, timely story told by one of our very best reporters, Luna Ortega." She smiled at Luna across the stage, and the crowd applauded. "Luna's story on our dependency on social media blew me away—and also gave credit to each and every one of the people who participated in the Offline October challenge. And tonight we're recognizing those participants."

I glanced toward the parking lot, but my feet didn't move. Frantically, I looked back at the stage in time to see Luna step up to Ms. Spencer's side. This was going to happen. I couldn't make it stop.

"Luna, why don't you say a few words about the challenge?" Ms. Spencer said. "You of all people know this wasn't as easy as it seemed."

Luna reached for the mic. "I'm not going to stand here and lie to you all."

The knife twisted in my stomach.

Luna beamed at the audience. "There have been plenty of times I've been tempted to log on to ChitChat this month. But thanks to all the support from my friends, I kept my vow. Now, I'm excited to share with you the participants in the Offline Challenge and tell you *exactly* how well they've done without one of the most popular social media apps—ChitChat." Dramatically, Luna held up the envelopes to show the audience. Lizzie and Kiyana stood to one side with a stack of papers in their hands. "As I read off your name, please come forward and some of our SO team members will give you a special certificate."

"Cheri Thomas . . ." Luna opened the first envelope. "According to ChitChat, you've been off the app for three days."

The crowd clapped politely, and Cheri bounced across the stage to take a piece of paper from Lizzie.

"Davis Jenkins . . . fourteen days."

The football players made loud whooping sounds from the back, and Davis went up to claim his award. He waved the sheet of paper over his head, and the cheers grew.

"Isco Mercado . . . sixteen days."

Isco bumped his fist into Milo's, then headed up the steps of the stage. Luna held out the award toward him cradled in her arms like it was an Academy Award statue. Isco took it, then leaned in to speak quickly into the microphone. "I want to thank my mom and everyone who made this possible."

Luna fake-kicked him off the stage, and everyone laughed.

But not me. I couldn't even focus on the fact that Isco had looked cute.

My turn was coming up fast. I glanced around in panic and saw Caitlin. If I couldn't come clean with Luna, I could at least tell Caitlin before everyone else knew. I pushed my way through the crowd toward her.

"I need to talk to you," I said, ignoring the press of the football team around her and Luna announcing the names in the background. I had to get this out now.

"I know," Caitlin said, looking confused. "We talked before, Annie. It's all okay. Remember?"

"No, not that." I tried to get her full attention, but she looked past me toward the stage.

"Luna's waving at us to get up there," she said. "We better go."

The comments kept scrolling in my head.

NOBODY LIKES YOU

SHE'S A TOTAL FRAUD

HAHAHAHAHAHAHAHA!!!!!!!!

"And now, for the biggest winners of all . . ." Luna paused and waved us onstage. Caitlin went first. I wanted to go in the opposite direction, as far away as possible, but I followed. I didn't know what else to do. A bright white light turned on at the top of the television camera in front of the stage.

Tamar walked out on the stage and took over the mic. "Before you call out these last names, I want to say something."

A tiny glimmer of hope appeared. Maybe somehow this would end. Luna stepped back beside me and Caitlin.

"I wanted to give one special shout-out before we run out of time tonight." Tamar looked over her shoulder to smile at Luna. "Luna has really stepped up her game with this timely story. I had a chance to read her wonderful article about it, and I hope you'll all help me congratulate her on becoming . . . our paper's new editor in chief!"

I glanced over in shock at Tamar, who gave Luna a thumbs-up and huge grin. "Congratulations!" Caitlin cried, grabbing Luna in a hug.

I wanted to hug Luna, too, but my arms felt too weak. Besides, Luna was already stepping back to the podium for Tamar's handshake and the crowd's applause. Everything seemed to be happening in slow motion.

"I know these last two names are important," Tamar added. "But you're right up there with them."

"Thank you so much," Luna told Tamar. She beamed at the television camera in front of her, then leaned into the microphone.

"Caitlin Stone . . ." Luna opened the next to last envelope in her hand. "Twenty-four days."

Caitlin made her way up to the podium, smiling. Cheers erupted across the field.

"Now for our last, but certainly not least, participant . . ." Luna reached back to pull me up by her side.

"Annie Webb . . ."

I'm a horrible friend.

Luna opened the envelope.

I couldn't breathe, no matter how much air I tried to gulp into my lungs.

She looked down at the paper, confused, then back at me like she wanted me to explain.

I can't keep a promise.

She covered the mic with one hand. "This must be a mistake," she said to me.

I shook my head, mute.

Her expression steeled; then she turned back to the microphone. "Two days."

The crowd let out a rumble of surprise. Luna's hand dropped from my shoulder, and I stood there alone. It suddenly felt like I was floating above myself.

"I'm so sorry," I whispered to Luna. "I tried to tell you."

She turned to face me, her hands clenched at her sides. "You didn't try hard enough."

Tamar, sensing that there was something wrong, quickly stepped up and took Luna's position at the mic. I heard her saying something to the crowd but couldn't make out her words. I could also feel Caitlin hovering nearby, watching me and Luna.

"Please listen," I begged Luna. "I wanted to be the kind of person who could leave ChitChat behind. But I couldn't. It's in my head all the time." Tears filled my eyes. "I'm sorry."

Luna's face closed up like blinds snapping down on the windowpane. I was outside. "You broke the vow."

I nodded. I had. And it was much worse than when Caitlin had done it.

Without saying anything else, Luna turned and hurried off the stage. Caitlin went after her, and didn't look back at me. I could tell the time wasn't right for me to follow them.

But I couldn't stay here either, among all these people. I had to escape.

CHAPTER TWENTY-SIX

Dogs do speak, but only to those who know how to listen.

—Orhan Pamuk

I didn't know where to go, but I needed to talk to someone, and he was the only one I knew who would listen without judgment.

"We're going to be closing up in just a few minutes," the woman behind the desk at the animal shelter told me as soon as I came inside.

"I won't be long."

Rocco stood at the door to his kennel like he knew I was coming, his tail wagging. I opened the gate and slipped inside, bending down to accept his kisses on my wet cheeks. Slowly I sank to the ground, and he crawled into my lap as best he could. I put my arms around his neck and buried my face in his soft fur, finally letting the tears come freely. Rocco leaned in, heavy and comforting against my chest.

"I should have told them," I mumbled against his throat. "I chose all those horrible people on ChitChat to follow rather than the people who actually cared about me. What's wrong with me?"

I pulled back from Rocco and settled cross-legged on

the concrete floor. He lay down at my side, head on my thigh. I rubbed his soft ears, and he made a low rumble of pleasure in his throat. The sound calmed me, and the tears slowed. Rocco rolled his eyes up to look at my face, but kept his chin planted firmly on my leg.

"I felt like if I didn't go on ChitChat I was missing out on something important, when the things that were most important were right there in front of me." Rocco gently put one huge paw on my foot as a gentle reminder to keep rubbing his ears while I talked. I obediently started petting him again. "I know it doesn't make sense."

"I thought I'd find you here," I heard a familiar voice say. I looked up to see Isco standing at the gate. "Can I come in?" he asked.

I nodded, quickly brushing my tears off with the shoulder of my sweater.

Isco settled on the floor beside me. "How are you doing?"

"I think you probably figured that out from what happened onstage at the Fall Festival."

"Yeah." Isco reached out to rub Rocco's back and was rewarded with a tail wag.

"I screwed up."

Isco shrugged. "It happens sometimes," he said. "To everybody."

"Staying on ChitChat was bad, but lying was even worse. Especially to my best friends."

"If they're your friends, they will understand. Tell them how you feel."

"How?" I frowned. "I don't even know where to start."

"You'll figure it out," Isco said. "I know you will."

I stroked Rocco's head, and his eyes closed in delight. If only people were so simple to please.

"Speaking of telling people how you feel . . ." Isco squinted one eye at me. "I didn't mean to come on too strong the other day."

"You didn't," I said.

He looked surprised. "I didn't?"

I shook my head. "No . . . I wanted to kiss you, actually. But I just wasn't ready. I was still getting over my ex-boyfriend, and dealing with everything happening online. But I think things are getting better now. I hope." A smile started very slowly on his lips and grew into full-blown Isco brilliance. My breath caught in my throat. And I smiled back.

The overhead lights blinked twice, signaling the shelter was closing. I stood up, giving Rocco a couple of goodbye pats.

Isco looked up at me, his dark eyes shining. "So, when you're ready, you'll let me know?"

I bit my bottom lip and nodded slowly. "But I need some time to try to fix the mess I made."

"I'll be here," Isco said, and I believed him.

○ ○ ○

I stopped at home first to pick up something, then went straight to Caitlin's house. Coach Stone answered the door and gave me a sad smile.

"Congratulations on the big win," I said.

"Thanks." He didn't move out of the way and invite me in like usual.

"I was hoping I could talk to Caitlin?" I hated the way my voice quivered.

"I'm sorry, Annie." He shook his head. "She said she didn't want to talk to you tonight."

I was stunned. In all our years of being best friends, this had never happened before. "Is Luna with her?"

He nodded. "Normally, I'd take you upstairs and get you all to figure things out face-to-face, but Cait was pretty upset. I think you might need to give her some space."

I looked away, blinking hard. Then I dug down into my bag to pull out the journal I'd grabbed from my room at home. The gold dragon on the front shone in the porchlight. "Can you give her this?"

Coach Stone looked down at the journal with raised eyebrows but didn't ask any questions. "I'll give it to her, but I can't promise anything," he said. He took the journal from my outstretched hand.

I turned to go back to my house, but he stopped me. "Just give it a little time, Annie. She'll talk to you."

"Thanks," I whispered.

○   ○   ○

Dad and Mom were on the couch laughing at a *Big Bang Theory* rerun, but I managed to hold my tears in long enough to greet them and get up the stairs before they looked my way.

I shut my bedroom door and flung myself across the bed, replaying all the shocked looks after the big announcement. But the faces that kept coming up over and over in my mind belonged to Caitlin and Luna. I lost my best friends because of my own stupidity. I sobbed so hard I couldn't catch my breath. Finally, I lay exhausted and still sniffling on my bed, staring up at the Eiffel Tower. I let out a long ragged breath. I didn't want to only see pictures of the Eiffel Tower. I wanted the real thing, but that meant seeing the real around me.

When did I stop listening to my real friends?

Is this who I want to be?

I glanced at my phone. The prison doors were still open, and it was time to leave.

One by one I deleted my social media accounts. Even the ones in my hidden folders where only I knew they were. Then I changed into my pajamas, brushed my teeth, and crawled back into bed, getting under the covers. My brain raced with worry, fear, and anxiety. But I didn't reach for my phone to shut down my thoughts.

I tossed and turned most of the night, but finally fell asleep toward morning. By the time I stumbled downstairs, sunshine lit up the family room through the open windows.

Savanna sat on the couch wrapped in a blanket and flipping through channels on the television. My dad sat at the dining room table, reading the paper.

"Ahh," Savanna said, seeing me. "Sleeping Beauty finally decides to join us."

I rubbed my eyes and squinted at her. She patted the

couch cushion beside her, and I obediently stumbled across the room in my oversized T-shirt, pj bottoms, and bare feet to plop down next to her. Out of habit, I had my cell phone in my hand, but I didn't check it.

"You look grumpy," Savanna said, throwing part of the blanket across my lap. I wanted to say if she'd lost her best friends, she would be grumpy, too. But I didn't.

"Do you want to talk about it?" she asked.

I shook my head.

"I know something to cheer you up."

"Does it involve weddings?" I asked.

She made a face. "Sort of . . ." She clicked the remote to the movies selection. "But not *my* wedding. Because we're all sick of talking about that, right?"

I looked at her in surprise. "Really?"

She shrugged. "I just need to think of something else for a while."

"Me too," I said, and Savanna laughed.

"So . . . let's watch a movie together. Your favorite. *The Princess Bride.*"

I smiled, even though I didn't think it possible today. "As you wish," I said.

We snuggled down in the blankets, pulling up throw cushions for pillows, and Savanna started the movie.

My dad joined us. "I haven't seen this in a long time. Can you pause it long enough for me to make some popcorn?"

Savanna giggled. "As you wish."

Dad popped the corn and then sprinkled it with his

special cheese mix. Within a few minutes, we were chanting along to our favorite lines and laughing at the best parts. Watching a movie you loved was almost as good as learning about faraway places. For a moment, the world of broken vows and shattered friendships slipped away.

"Those sea snake things terrify me," Mom said. I didn't even realize she had come into the room and was standing behind the couch in her scrubs. She walked around and sat down beside Dad, putting up her feet on the coffee table and snuggling into his shoulder. I passed the bowl of popcorn in her direction, still chewing. It felt good to be a family—just the four of us—for a little while longer.

I could only think of one more thing that could add to this scene.

"I think we should get a dog," I said.

"Very funny," Mom said, then put a handful of popcorn in her mouth.

But I wasn't kidding. And of course I had a very specific dog in mind.

Just as the movie finished, my phone buzzed with a text message. I reached for my phone warily, and what I saw on the screen surprised me.

LUNA: LOOK OUT YOUR WINDOW

CHAPTER TWENTY-SEVEN

Friendship is the only cement that will hold the world together.

—Woodrow Wilson

I rushed upstairs to my room and pulled back the curtain, staring out toward Luna's bedroom. But her blinds were closed tight. There was no welcoming figure signaling me to come over. My heart sank. Maybe the text had been some sort of a cruel trick, although that wasn't Luna's style.

But just before I shut my curtains, I saw the flicker in the distance. The firepit in Caitlin's backyard was lit. The smoke curled up into the sky, sending out a signal of hope.

I threw on leggings, a hoodie, and my sneakers. I left my phone sitting on my desk. When I entered the backyard a few minutes later, I found Luna and Caitlin sitting around the fire.

"Hey," Luna said when she saw me. "We were hoping you'd come."

My heart pounded with nerves, but I was relieved she said that. I glanced at Caitlin, and she nodded.

I dropped down in the Adirondack chair next to Luna, stretching my legs out in front of me. I waited for one of them to say something, but it was quiet except for the crackling of the recently lit fire. Flames licked out around the pile of wood in the middle of the stone circle, blue in the center and bright white in the flickers. Heat washed across my face, and I scooted closer, holding out my hands to the warmth. We sat in silence for a few more minutes, all of us watching the fire. I thought of all the times we'd lit fires and all the reasons.

Finally, I said, "I'm sorry."

The words were quiet and small, but I couldn't add anything else to them. I hoped it was enough.

"I was reading." Luna held up my journal, and I realized she'd been holding it in her lap. She motioned toward Caitlin. "We both were."

My mouth quivered. This was not what I expected. My heart raced while I waited for what would come next.

"I didn't know how hard the vow was for you," Luna said. "I mean, it was hard for all of us. But . . ."

I turned toward her and sighed. "I know. It shouldn't have taken me this long to tell you. And you shouldn't have found out the way you did. I never meant to let you down."

"But why couldn't you tell us in person what you wrote in the journal?" Caitlin asked.

I shook my head. "I don't know. Without ChitChat, it felt like I wasn't real," I said. "And I felt like I was missing out on too much. And that felt silly to admit to you guys."

"You can tell us anything," Luna said. "Even if it's silly. You know that, right?"

Big, fat tears gathered in my eyes. I nodded.

"Besides, it's not silly," Luna said. "Caitlin and I felt the same way."

"I mean, come on," Caitlin chimed in. "I broke the vow, too. I get it."

Luna nodded. "It's hard, what we did. We can't put too much pressure on ourselves."

I thought about what Isco had said. "Yeah. Everybody makes mistakes." I looked at Caitlin. "Me . . . you . . . Milo."

I saw the hope in her eyes.

"If you want to give him a chance, I won't stand in the way," I told her.

"Okay," Caitlin agreed, giving a shaky laugh.

I let out a breath of relief. "What I really want to say is that the worst part was not breaking the vow. It was not being honest with you both," I said. I looked from Caitlin to Luna.

Luna reached out and squeezed my hand. "Your journal was so powerful," Luna said. "It made me remember why I love words so much. Maybe one day—when you're ready—I can share your *real* story about ChitChat? I think there are lots of people who need to read it."

I nodded. "I'll think about it."

"Here." Caitlin held out her journal to me. "Feel free to read my journal. It's a scary thing handing this over. You must have been terrified. There are things in here I haven't told anyone. Anyway . . ."

I could feel my hand shaking as I reached for it. "Are you sure?"

She nodded.

"You should have this one, too." Luna gave me her journal as well.

I felt the weight of both in my hands. Light. Easy. Yet so full of thoughts never shared.

"I don't deserve this," I said, blinking back tears.

"Nobody *deserves* best friends," Luna said. "That's exactly why they are there when you need them."

Now I was smiling inside and out. Caitlin stood up to throw another log on the fire, and the flames grew. I watched the light flicker and glow on the faces around the circle.

"Can we say it?" I asked.

Then we all chanted together in unison.

"As this fire is my witness, I vow to always stay friends. No matter what. No matter how."

ᯓ ᯓ ᯓ

Later that afternoon, I went grocery shopping with my dad. I felt so much lighter and freer after talking with Luna and Caitlin, but there was still something big on my mind.

"Hey, Dad? Do you remember when we were watching the movie . . . ?" I began.

"Uh-huh," he said, looking up and down the row of cottage cheese. I could tell he wasn't paying attention. He held out one brand, brow furrowed. "Is this the one your mom likes?"

"Sure," I said, even though I really didn't know. "And remember how I said we needed a dog?"

He rolled the cart toward the lunch meat and picked up some honey-baked turkey. "You don't like dogs."

I casually added some string cheese to the basket. "That's the thing. I *thought* I didn't like dogs, but actually I do. A lot. "

"Okay," my dad said. "Maybe one day you'll get a dog."

I stood in front of the cart, keeping it from rolling any farther. "I like this one dog in particular."

Suddenly, it dawned on him. He shook his head emphatically, then rolled the cart around me. "No way, Annie. We're not getting a dog. There is enough going on in our house with Savanna's wedding. We definitely don't need a dog!"

"I'll take care of everything," I promised. "I'll feed the dog, and walk him, and buy his food and take him to the vet. Promise." I also had a plan, one that I'd texted Isco about earlier. If I could get a part-time job at the shelter, that would give me enough money to pay for Rocco's dog food and vet visits. I'd thought of everything.

"None of us have the time to train a dog." Dad shifted his attention to the man behind the counter and ordered a pound of ground meat.

"That's the great thing about Rocco," I said. "He's already trained. He knows all his commands and he's an older dog, so no puppy craziness."

My dad accepted the package from the butcher and rolled off toward the bread aisle. I followed closely. Dad put a loaf of bread in the cart. I took his silence as a good sign.

"Rocco is a really great dog, Dad." I put my hand on his and looked him straight in the eyes. "And this is important to me."

He looked back at me, then said, "Your mom's going to kill me."

I jumped up and down, screaming and hugging him right in the middle of the fruits and vegetables.

⏻   ⏻   ⏻

Bright and early on Sunday, Dad drove me to the shelter.

Somehow, Rocco knew when I snapped the leash onto his collar that today was different. That we weren't just going out for a quick walk and coming back. He looked up at me with all-knowing eyes, smiling his happy, panting grin. His tail thumped against the concrete rhythmically—*thump, thump, thump*—but there were no excited twirls or whines. It was as though he always knew this day would come and wondered why it had taken so long for me to realize it.

"We're going home," I told him, and we walked down the long corridor and out the front door of the shelter. Isco wasn't working today, but I waved to the woman behind the desk, the one who'd helped me and Dad out with all the paperwork. If everything panned out, I'd be back here myself to work someday soon.

⏻   ⏻   ⏻

I opened the front door, and Rocco walked into the house, tail wagging and sniffing at the scents. Slowly he made his way into the kitchen, and I showed him his very own bowl—one I had purchased yesterday—on the floor by the pantry. Then I gave him a new toy, a stuffed elephant. He carried it in his mouth as we explored the rest of the house, including the upstairs bedrooms and his new dog pillow in the corner of my room. Finally, there was the backyard. Rocco explored every corner from one side of the fence to the other, checking in with me every few minutes to make sure I was still there. I sat on the patio steps and watched his joy. I could see it from his panting smiley face to the tip of his wildly wagging tail—this was a wonderful, astonishing place. He joined me on the steps with a lick of a kiss. I put my arm around his shoulders, and we surveyed his new world with satisfaction.

"There's even a squirrel that comes down that pine tree and walks right down the top of the fence," I told him.

When Mom came downstairs from sleeping, Dad and I were settled in on the family room floor playing with Rocco and Elephant. Rocco lifted his head, Elephant between his front paws, and just waited. Mom sat in the chair opposite us, her face grim.

"So this is Rocco?"

I nodded.

Mom ever so slightly patted the side of her leg. Rocco immediately got up and crossed the room, leaving Elephant behind at my feet.

"Sit," Mom said.

Rocco sat.

Mom looked at Rocco. Rocco looked at Mom.

"Do you think you're going to be happy here?" Mom asked Rocco.

Rocco's tail smacked against the floor in response.

"Me too," Mom said, then reached out to scratch Rocco right on the spot behind his ears where he liked it best. He lay down, then rolled over for tummy rubs. Mom obliged. I grinned.

By later that afternoon, the whole family was like putty in Rocco's paws. He let Savanna dress him up in a baseball hat and sunglasses. He listened intently to my mom's favorite jazz station and kept time with his tail. He even snuggled in, at my father's invitation, on the couch to watch a science documentary.

After, we went up to my room. I congratulated Rocco on a job well done, but he just put his big head on my stomach and began to snore. I took a photo of him and texted it to Isco, who responded right away with a bunch of exclamation points. He was thrilled I'd adopted Rocco, and we texted back and forth for a while. But I didn't stay on my phone for long. I put it aside, stroked Rocco's soft brown nose, and stared up at the Eiffel Tower on my ceiling.

Journeys don't always go as intended, I thought. And maybe that was the best thing.

◐　◐　◐

ME: ROCCO WANTS TO MEET THE REST OF MY FAMILY. ☺ MEET AT THE PARK IN 10 MINUTES?

CAITLIN: SEE YOU THERE!

LUNA: ON MY WAY.

When we met up with Caitlin and Luna, Rocco's tail waved so wildly it shook his whole back end. He knew all the attention was for him, and he loved it.

"He's so big," Luna said, squatting down to kiss him firmly on the nose.

"And soft." Caitlin stroked the top of his head.

Rocco looked from one to the other as though this was the best moment of his life, but he always looked like that since he'd left the shelter. I parked myself on the bench at the picnic table, the sun warming my back, and Rocco lay at my feet. The park was deserted except for the three of us, but that wasn't unusual. The developers put it in before they built more houses at the end of our street, so for now it sat alone in the middle of a wide field of grass with only three swings, a slide, and one picnic table.

Caitlin sat on the swing and let her feet dangle onto the rocks below. Luna pushed herself out of the opening at the top of the slide and slid down, arms outstretched over her head.

I walked over to join Caitlin on the swings. "Thanks for trusting me with your journal," I told her. "I didn't know how you felt about your father. It helped me understand what you've been going through after your mom died."

Caitlin nodded. "This whole vow thing wasn't all bad," she said. "At least it led to the journals."

"Of course it wasn't." I looked at Luna. "And you wrote an amazing article because of it. One that connected with so many people. But I didn't know until I read your journal how much pressure you put on yourself."

Luna sighed. "It's true." She walked over and sat on the last swing.

Rocco watched us from his spot in the shade, grinning happily, his tongue out. I pushed off into the space before me, feeling the crisp air on my face. I pumped my legs and soared back out and up. The view of the foothills was eye level now, and the white-tipped peaks were in stark contrast to the brilliant blue afternoon sky.

"And I learned . . ." I said as the swing brought me back to earth. "To be here right now."

Together we swung back and forth, not saying anything for a long time. Sometimes it seemed we knew each other so well we didn't have to make explanations or apologies. But sometimes, there were whispers of everything we didn't say.

"Are you going to go back to ChitChat?" Caitlin asked me after a few minutes.

I looked down and stopped the swing's momentum by letting my feet drag through the rocks. "Not for a while. If

I go back, I want to make sure I control how I use it and it doesn't control me," I said. "How about you guys?"

"Not yet, but I probably will," Caitlin said. "I think I'll just be more aware of how much I'm missing out on in real life when I spend too much time on ChitChat."

I nodded. "Yeah. Me too."

Luna was still swinging. "I've already gone back," she called out from the top of the arc. Gradually, her swings grew smaller until she stopped beside us. "But it feels different now. Like you said—it doesn't control me."

"I heard Mariah posted a video of Discord's whole performance at the Fall Festival," Caitlin said, then looked at me like she might have said something wrong.

I rolled my eyes. "It's okay."

Strangely enough, Mariah didn't matter. Maybe it was because I hadn't gone on ChitChat since before the Fall Festival. I no longer knew what shoes she wore or what she ate for dinner. I didn't know the name of the perfume she bought. I felt completely and utterly disconnected from her. And that was a very good thing. I could also think about Jameson now without feeling jealous or sad. I really had moved on from him.

"How about we do a 'Phone Stays Home' night tomorrow?" Luna suggested. "There's this new burger place that just opened up on Walnut."

"I can't," I admitted, feeling a blush start in my cheeks. Rocco padded over to me and curled up at my feet.

"Why not? You got something better to do?" Luna asked.

Reaching down to avoid eye contact, I stroked Rocco's head. His tail thumped in response.

Caitlin immediately jumped on my uncomfortable response. "You do!"

"It's not *better*," I clarified, "but . . . I asked Isco to go salsa dancing."

"That's amazing," Luna declared. "Is it like . . . a date?"

I shrugged, blushing even more. "I don't think so, yet. We're friends. But . . . maybe?"

We all three giggled like we were twelve again and had just discovered our first crush. I'd forgotten what that felt like.

"But the burger place the next night?" I offered. "Just the three of us?"

"And Rocco can come, too," Caitlin said. "I think they're pet friendly."

"Perfect," I said.

I reached my hands across the space between the swings, holding out my palms. Caitlin took one side and Luna the other. Together we synchronized, swinging in unison. The sun was lower in the sky now and a new chill in the air nipped at our faces, leaving bright pink spots high on our cheeks.

For a moment, I wished for someone to come along to take a photo of the three of us. I would have liked to document this moment. Then I sighed, realizing my brain still had some old habits to break.

I swung and watched the wind move the tops of the

red-and-gold aspen trees, their leaves sounding like rushing water all around us. A dusting of snow covered the foothills in the distance, and beyond that the craggy peaks of the Rocky Mountains jutted into the bright blue sky.

The three of us didn't need to record this moment.

We just needed to live it.

TURN THE PAGE FOR A SNEAK
PEEK AT ANOTHER RIVETING
BOOK BY DONNA COONER!

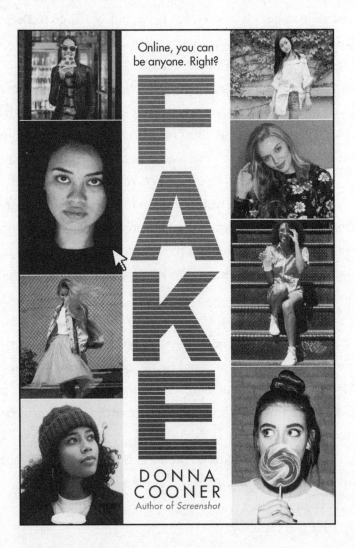

Online, you can
be anyone. Right?

FAKE

DONNA
COONER
Author of *Screenshot*

I shut down the computer. The black screen becomes a mirror. Instead of Bella's and Camila's gorgeous smiles, I only see my own fat, sad face. No matter what all the self-help mantras say, I am not enough.

I put the laptop on my nightstand, turn off the lights, and slide under my covers. I'm tired, but I can't go to sleep. Instead, I toss and turn, rearranging blankets and changing positions over and over. Finally, I end up on my back staring up at the ceiling, my hands clenched in fists by my side. I think about the meme of me sitting down on the stool next to Jesse. The ChitChats from the party replay in my mind like a movie projected onto my bedroom ceiling.

Why am I here in this world? There has to be a reason.

I want to believe I would step up to push the child away from the speeding car, to rescue the drowning puppy, to walk the old woman across the street. I *want* to believe it. But how can I be a hero when I don't even stand up for myself?

I understand cowards. They didn't start out that way. Something changed them. At some point something horrible met them as they stepped up to confront their demons. Maybe it wasn't all at once. Sometimes the demons chip away at you, whispering and slithering their way into the strongest of hearts.

There is a tiny spark of something I don't want to face here with me in the dark.

It is anger.

And it is growing.

A tiny voice begins to whisper in some small part of my brain. It gets deeper and louder until I finally know exactly what to do. The thought takes hold and starts to grow.

Jesse Santos is only one member of the popular crowd. I can't take them all down, but he has a target on his back. Maybe I can't be the one to defeat him in my current form, but what if I shape-shifted into something else?

Or *someone* else?

I might be able to wipe that stupid grin off his face. Maybe I could actually make him care about something other than football practice and being cool and making fat girls like me miserable.

Minute electrical sparks tingle at my nerves. Adrenaline courses through my veins.

Wonder Woman doesn't fight evil as Diana.

Superman doesn't right wrongs as Clark Kent.

They change.

I sit up and turn on the light. My eyes wander over to where my comic strips hang on my wall. Dragons with glasses. Elephants with porcupine skins. Fairies with cell phones. Unbelievable creatures I can never become when all I really want to change into is a perfectly normal-looking teenage girl. A completely impossible dream.

Or is it?

I sit frozen, thinking. Katy Purry bumps her head against my hand. I rub the spot under her chin where I know she likes it most, and then I pull my computer off my nightstand. My mind races. The idea is still bubbling inside my brain. I think it over, scratching Katy Purry behind one ear. It is so wrong on so many levels and yet . . .

This is crazy.

Crazy awesome.

I turn my computer back on and open ChitChat. The best place for this little experiment to go down. I find the button for *Create New Profile.*

The empty screen with the blinking cursor makes me feel the same way I do when I look at the blank frame in my comic strip—powerful and invincible. There is going to be something here soon that has never existed before, and I am going to be the one to create it.

I quickly discover lying—I mean *creating*—online isn't complicated. It's like drawing a new character for one of my strips, but instead I use my keyboard. First, I need a name. Something cool and a little bit unusual. My eyes wander over to my desk. The soft reddish-brown color of one of my markers speaks to me. It makes sense that my creation should emerge from the colors I use for my drawings.

Sienna.

I write in the new profile name—Sienna Maras. Even her last name has special meaning to me. In some Scandinavian shape-shifting tales I read once, the Maras are restless children whose souls leave their bodies at night to haunt the living.

So appropriate.

Now Sienna needs a bio. Something catchy. I spend the next thirty minutes researching different websites and celebrity social media accounts. Finally, I write, *"Be yourself. Everyone else is taken."*

It's my own little inside joke. An Easter egg planted, but only for me.

I give Sienna's age—sixteen—and her location: Denver. Close, but not too close.

And now the most important part.

The picture.

I start to search on ChitChat for images of random girls, but looking for my perfect replacement makes me bitter. The more pretty girl pictures I see, the angrier I get. So many likes and comments. So much praise. They live in a world I will never know. I feel the anxiety rising in my throat, choking me.

Telling me to be okay with my body through perky Pinterest statements and Dove commercials doesn't change the way I feel inside. If I'm honest with myself, I would unzip my skin and step out of it. Just for a day. An hour. For a break. A breath.

Don't ever admit that to anyone.

For now, I give up on finding Sienna's perfect face. The picture is crucial, and I'll take my time finding just the right one, even if it takes me all weekend.

Then, still in Sienna's profile, I click over to Jesse's

page and hit the *Send Direct Message* button. I take a deep breath. This is it.

For every oink.

For every giggle.

For every eye roll.

For every turned back.

For every stupid meme.

For every broken heart.

A shape-shifter steps out of the shadows and takes up the challenge.

Stories that feel true-to-life from
DONNA COONER

Someone has taken an incriminating photo of Skye and is threatening to leak it everywhere...

When Maisie decides to create a fake online profile, everything spins out of control.

Everyone at Linden's school is obsessed with a new app, Worthy, which judges couples. And then the app focuses on Linden and her boyfriend...

Torrey is a beauty and fashion vlogger with tons of fans. But when her sister dies, Torrey's offscreen world implodes.

Ever undergoes a drastic elective surgery—but she still has to do battle with the insecurity that haunts her.

I read YA

IReadYA.com

DCOONER5